FATHER'S DAY

GARY KYRIAZI

outskirts
press

*To Aunt Virginia,
for a lifetime of
encouragement and support*

This story took place
on Father's Day weekend in 1984.

ONE

Pastor Salvatore Satori walked south down the middle of State Highway 1 that served as the main street for La Sangre, California. The sun had just risen, and there was no traffic on the winding, two-lane coastal route. But soon, out-of-state tourists and regional weekend motorists would be traveling up the coast from San Francisco, lazily absorbing Highway 1's world famous views of the Pacific Ocean, the varied pastoral scenes of cattle and sheep, and the occasional small towns that advertised antique stores and bed-and-breakfast inns. Some of the drivers would stop in La Sangre for gas at the two-pump La Sangre Last Chance Gas Station and Garage, or for soft drinks and munchies at the La Sangre Grocery Store, for firewood and sundry supplies at the La Sangre General Store, perhaps to browse in the La Sangre Antique Store, and maybe to have breakfast or lunch at the La Sangre Saloon, subtitled "Good Food."

Sal winced, as he did every morning on his walk, at the rustic wooden Old West false front of the La Sangre Saloon, and he wondered, as he did every morning, if he should replace the word "Saloon" with "Diner." Although alcohol hadn't been served there since Sal had taken over the town 12 years ago, any such change would require permission from the California Coastal Commission. While such a minor change would likely be approved by the CCC, as it wouldn't in any way mar the well-protected beauty of the California coast, Sal preferred as little interaction with them as possible. Even something as innocuous as changing "Saloon" to "Diner" would call undue attention to the town. The CCC was always content with La Sangre's consistency, and Sal was determined to keep it that way. Besides, the Saloon did attract drivers, and while they were invariably disappointed they couldn't at least buy a beer, once they had gone to the trouble of pulling over, they usually bought something to eat, and often walked next door or across the road to browse in the other charming false Western-front buildings.

Sal stopped in the middle of the road, his feet firmly planted on each side of the double yellow no-passing line. He was proud of how he maintained control over La Sangre and its one hundred residents, and how God continued to bless them. God had answered all of Sal's prayers; Sal had seen to that.

"Good morning Pastor!" called a rough voice.

"Praise the Lord!"

Sal looked fifty feet north on the road to where Doyle Seeno, tall, lean, and yes, mean, to outsiders anyway, was unlocking the gas pumps. Sal paused before responding, establishing his authority. He did that a lot with Doyle.

"Doyle," Sal finally nodded slowly, maintaining his stance in the middle of the road.

"The Lord gave us a beautiful morning, didn't He?"

"Yes. He did."

"Should be a lot of traffic up and down the coast this weekend. Folks'll be needin' gas. After all, it's 36 miles from Bodega Bay south, and 80 miles north to Fort Bragg. Folks'll be needin' gas."

As if Sal needed to be reminded of the mileage. He smiled as he thought about how the La Sangre Last Chance Gas Station charged one dollar per gallon more than the stations in either of those towns. Still, people always filled up. Slow driving on the curvy, cliffside Highway 1 intimidated first-timers, and a full tank of gas made them feel secure.

"Do we have enough gas?" Sal asked Doyle. He'd seen the truck arrive yesterday afternoon, but he was validating Doyle's limited authority.

"Yes we do, Pastor. The Lord provided us with a shipment yesterday afternoon."

"Good."

Doyle Seeno savored the ritualistic morning conversations with Pastor Satori as one might a morning cup of coffee. At 47, Doyle had his world ordered and in control. Alone and desolate, he had responded to an ad in the Santa Rosa paper and arrived in town shortly after Sal had taken over the church, and eventually the town. Doyle found his place as a lay mechanic for the La Sangre Last Chance Gas Station and Garage, knowing enough to make minor repairs, and if necessary, call for a tow truck to take vehicles inland to the shops in Santa Rosa. He had a room upstairs from the gas station and a secure, daily routine. He was content and grateful to the Pastor and to the town. Someday he might even take a wife; someone clean and pure whom he could share his humble life with. Not like that little whore back in McCarthy, Texas, 32 years ago. She'll burn in hell, that one.

"Is the room ready?" Sal looked above the garage to the window on the right.

"It sure is, Pastor." Doyle followed Sal's gaze. "I cleaned it up good. Hope your boy doesn't mind sharing the bathroom with me."

"It'll be good for him, teach him some responsibility. It's the first step to get him out on his own. Mrs. Satori bought him a two-burner hot plate and a little refrigerator, so he can learn to cook his own meals. He's been spoiled for too long."

"A kid shouldn't be spoiled," Doyle agreed. "I had to work for everything. My daddy never spoiled me, beat me good when I needed it. No, don't you worry about your boy, Pastor. I'll keep an eye on him."

"Thank you Doyle," Sal nodded. It was a two-win situation: someone to keep an eye on his son, and another way of making Doyle feel needed, thereby strengthening Doyle's loyalty to him. "I'll see you in church tomorrow morning. And at the Father's Day picnic afterwards."

Doyle looked up, the morning fog was already beginning to burn off. "Should be a good day for the picnic. A good turnout."

"Yes, it should be," Sal nodded, and in dismissal, he turned his back on Doyle and resumed his walk southward down the middle of the road. A good turnout at the picnic meant the whole town, unless somebody was sick. Then, a few of the women would drop by the house of the infirmed with barbecued chicken, potato salad, and prayers for recovery. La Sangre looked after its own.

The last building south on his right, across from the Saloon, was the La Sangre General Store and Post Office. It was run by Lillian Walker, R.N., and in the rear of the store was a First Aid Station and Infirmary. Mature, wise, and unmarried, Sal considered Nurse Walker one of La Sangre's finest citizens, and he made sure she was taken care of financially from the church's tithes. He appreciated her humbled resignation and her plain, sexless, late-forties demeanor. One time he found himself looking at her barely discernible breasts, wondering what they would look like uncovered, but he immediately squelched the thought and asked for forgiveness.

Sal was in his late-thirties, with black hair, olive skin, and a rich baritone voice that could surround the beholder with a warm Italian/ Mediterranean climate. He had a solid buffalo build: all chest and arms, tapering to a slim waist, with short, strong legs. When he walked, each step was firm and carried more than his 190 pounds, as if he could, at will, implant himself into the earth. He was handsome, even down to his flattened nose, like that of a boxer. Everything that had been given to Sal, including and perhaps especially, his flat nose, Sal knew how to use.

Just as he reached the south end of the town, marked on the eastern shoulder with the highway sign reading "La Sangre: Elevation 75 feet, Population 100," he stopped suddenly. He usually walked further, at least 100 feet beyond the sign, so he could turn around and take pleasure in reading the sign as a motorist would.

But something was different this morning. He could tell. He could feel it. But what?

He again planted his feet on either side of the double yellow line, preparing for battle. He considered the events of the morning. As usual, he'd risen ahead of his wife, had dressed in khakis and a polo shirt, and gone outside, perusing the bluff and the ocean from his deck. Everything was in order. He'd taken the path that led south from his house on the north end of La Sangre through several modest oceanside homes to the dirt road that ran east from the bluff to Highway 1. He'd walked up the dirt road, then turned south on Highway 1 through the town, and had his usual exchange with Doyle. Everything was under control there, certainly no problem with Doyle.

And yet something was, not just different, but wrong.

Sal turned around, exchanging the position of his feet on each side of the yellow line, and looked north, back at his town, at the five buildings on either side of Highway 1: the Saloon, Gas Station, and Antique Store on the right, the General Store and Grocery Store on the left. Further up the highway, on the left, stood the La Sangre Christian Church. There were no strange cars along the highway; in fact, no cars at all. Only a few people in La Sangre owned cars, and they kept them in detached, one-car garages next to their homes. The auto-less people used their garages, if they had one, for workshops or storage. The church had a van that served as transportation for them, usually taking them in to Santa Rosa for provisions.

Still, something was wrong. Sal knew it. He turned around and faced south, again planting his feet solidly. Unmistakably, he sensed trouble, coming from the south. San Francisco probably. Yes, he was sure of it. An attack by Satan, coming from the south. And it was God who was advising him so.

It didn't frighten him. In fact, Sal looked forward to the challenge. It was his job as Pastor of La Sangre to meet Satan head on and to crush him beneath his feet, like he would a rattlesnake about to strike. That was the reason the town had chosen him as Pastor 12 years ago, the reason everyone had unquestionably put their faith in him. They didn't have to be afraid of anything anymore. Pastor Salvatore Satori could and would handle Satan.

Having proclaimed his solid position on Highway 1 to the as yet unseen enemy, Sal walked over to the guard rail on the west side of the road. It embraced a left hairpin curve that occurred immediately after leaving La Sangre southbound. Just after Sal's arrival in La Sangre, the California State Department of Transportation had replaced the heavy wooden beams with galvanized steel, preventing "anything but a semi-truck from going over the edge," they assured him, "no matter how fast they're going." Sal smiled. Semi trucks never drove this section of Highway 1. Any large shipments unloaded in Santa Rosa and supplies were then transported by van into La Sangre. Caltrans must have known that, but he appreciated the new guard rail anyway.

At that time Caltrans had also lowered the speed limit warning sign for the left turn from its previous 20 miles per hour to 15 mph. Sal appreciated that also. Beyond the standard 25 mph for any town on Highway 1, northbound cars heeded the yellow 15 mph warning sign on the curve before entering La Sangre, and for southbound cars, the 15 mph sign was easily visible ahead. It kept traffic practically to a crawl, encouraging drivers to stop. La Sangre's children were as safe from traffic as they were from the cliff. No child went out onto the bluff or up by the road without supervision, and a rite of passage—as his son Corey had gone through—was to play on the bluff alone and cross Highway 1 alone. Just don't go too close to the cliff, and look both ways on the road.

But now there was a fight coming, from the south. In preparation for battle, Sal sat down on the steel guard rail, facing the ocean. He listened to its deep sound as it slammed against the bottom of the 75-foot cliff directly below him. Sal was at one with the ocean: it protected him and the town, warning them of anything threatening, anything evil.

So Pastor Salvatore Satori just listened, and knew everything would be all right. He was confident and unafraid that any trouble or troublemaker that came into his town would be confronted face to face by Sal himself, and then thrown over the cliff and dashed against the rocks below. Then, if the sinner was salvageable, he or she would be gently lifted from the rocks, bones broken, their blood cleansed by the salt water, and then brought lovingly to the Lord.

TWO

Peter Freeman was four years old, in an orchard, sitting on his father's wide shoulders, his small hands clasped around his father's forehead. His father was somehow taller than normal, like a superman, enabling Peter to see over the vast expanse of the orchard, which stretched for miles eastward from Bakersfield, California, to what he would later learn was the southern range of the Sierra Nevada.

"This is all ours, Pete," his father said. "This is Lawrence Freeman Produce."

"What's produce, Daddy?"

"Well, our produce is almonds and citrus."

"What's citrus?"

"Oranges and grapefruit mostly. Pete, we're one of the biggest produce growers in California, and California supplies 80% of the produce for the entire country. And someday..."

"Yes Daddy?"

"Someday son, it will be yours."

"Mine?"

"Yes son, yours."

Peter awoke with a gasp. He looked around at his bedroom, got his bearings, then exhaled.

Well, that dream was a no-brainer: he couldn't stall much longer, there was a phone call he had to make. Whatever his decision, he had to phone it in.

Otherwise the dream had been beautiful and pastoral, and even conciliatory.

Conciliatory. And that was enough to make Peter, finally, cry. Four days after his father's funeral and he finally cried. He hadn't been ashamed or afraid to cry when he got the phone call from his oldest sister, nor in front of the over five hundred people that had attended Lawrence Freeman's service and burial. Besides, Peter was too busy to even think about crying since the day of his father's death, as he attended to his mother and four younger sisters, and responded to the hundreds of well-wishers associated with his father, mostly through his company, Lawrence Freeman Produce. True to Peter's dream, "LFP" was one of the largest agricultural companies in California's Central Valley, certainly the largest in the Bakersfield area.

Peter had tearlessly delivered the eulogy that was written by the LFP Public Relations Department. It outlined Lawrence Freeman's legacy as an outstanding businessman, philanthropist, and community leader, a pillar of Bakersfield and the Central Valley. Somewhere tucked within the eulogy's wealth of superlatives was a mention that Lawrence Freeman had married his high school sweetheart, Grace, and they had five children together. Peter's football accomplishments, his Superbowl win, were also mentioned, as a credit to Lawrence's superior stock. The fact that the cause of death for 57-year-old Lawrence Freeman, the picture of health himself, was a heart attack, was omitted.

"This is a hard time for you, I know Pete," Lawrence Freeman's longtime CPA advised him at the luncheon following the funeral. "So take your time, go through the grief, and then let me know about taking your place, your father's place, in LFP. It's *your* LFP now."

Go through the grief? And just what was "grief?" Any feeling that Peter felt, or allowed himself to feel since his sister's phone call was an almost perfect mix: half of him felt a newfound freedom from the overwhelming demands and obligations, the other half was the fear of anchoring himself with his father's body in the freshly dug grave. He could choose between his own new, free life, or commit himself to his father's life, which would probably kill him at the age of 57, just 23 years ahead. ("Someday it will be yours," his father had said in the dream.) No contest. So what was this supposed "grief?"

But waking up this Saturday morning, the day before Father's Day, something— grief he supposed—had sucker-punched him, first with the dream and then waking up with the concrete knowledge that his father was actually dead.

So Peter lay in bed and cried for five minutes, deep gut-level tears. Actually it felt good, flushing him out. When was the last time he'd cried? When he was seventeen, he remembered it well. Seventeen years, half of his life ago. Had he been afraid to cry all those years? Or had there been nothing to cry about?

After the wrenching in his stomach subsided and the weight in his chest dissolved, Peter continued to lay in bed, figuring it out. It didn't take long. This mixture of undefined loss and undefined new beginning led to a new clarity: he wasn't crying for the loss of his father, but for what never was and could have/should have been.

All right, enough! Peter propped himself up on his elbows, in his mortgage-free, three-story condo that sat on San Francisco's Great Highway, facing the Pacific Ocean. All he has to do is make a phone call, and then on with his new life.

New life? He took a brief self-inventory: 34 years old, single, two-years-retired running back for the San Francisco Forty-Niners. He'll call LFP and just say no, like one of the Public Service Announcements he'd recently made on behalf of the First Lady ("Just say no to drugs!").

If he chose not to take over Dad's business, that was his choice, right? His mother and sisters certainly didn't expect that, and he doubted they'd expect him to fill his father's shoes in any case, not that anybody could. They had always let Peter be, always supported him, were there for him. His four sisters had all lived their lives in different reactions to their father's synonymous presence and absence. Two of them had married men whom Peter suspected they didn't really love. But then, what did he know? He knew less about love than about grief.

He threw back the covers, swung his legs out of bed and sat, resting his hands on his knees. He looked at the Superbowl XVI ring on the third finger of his right hand. He'd had a good run in the National Football League, literally and figuratively, longer than most running backs, and at age 32 he wisely retired. No serious injuries: his sports doctor referred to Peter's body as "miraculously elastic." But his knees were getting weaker and there was no point in pushing it. He didn't have to be talked out of retirement, not by owner Eddie DeBartolo, Jr., Coach Bill Walsh, his agent nor anybody else. It was Peter's time, and he knew it. Helping to win a Superbowl, the first ever for the San Francisco Forty-Niners, was a good way to go out.

Since retiring two years ago, Peter's agent was keeping him busy with endorsements, personal appearances, and some guest spots with the sportscasters. In the meantime, his father was asking him to return to Bakersfield and take his place in LFP. Lawrence Freeman was wisely not over-pressuring Peter; this was, after all, a business transaction, and Lawrence was expert at closing a deal. Peter kept stalling him...and stalling himself. In the meantime, his phone would ring, his agent would have a gig for him, a TV or personal appearance, an endorsement, and it would keep Peter busy. He visited schools, talked to and encouraged kids, appeared at Pop Warner games, and did his community duty. But he avoided any permanent offers, even sportscasting. Peter was handsome and articulate enough for that, made a good appearance on TV, but all permanent job offers were out of town, and he wasn't ready to even consider moving from his home on the Pacific Ocean. That was the only thing he was certain of: he loved his home and didn't want to move anywhere.

So, what are you going to do Peter? You've made a lot of money in the NFL and have managed it well. With moderate living you'll never have to work again. Your Mom won't mind if you don't take over the business, and your sisters have encouraged you to follow your heart.

Follow his heart. Therein lay the rub. Where was his heart?

Think Peter. It'll come to you.

During his ten years with the San Francisco Forty-Niners he never had this problem carrying the ball down field, finding his path naturally, without thinking about it. During the Superbowl one sportscaster commented that "Pete Freeman appears to create, at will, openings on the field, like Moses parting the Red Sea!" Peter had to smile at himself at that comment, and swiped the tears off his face with his wrist.

But his smile disappeared when he remembered comments from his father that "Joe Montana *is* the Forty-Niners. Because of him they're a passing team, not a running team.... well, except for Ricky Patton." His father had to throw that last part in. He always knew his trump line to close a deal. Romance the opponent and then deliver the final blow that would convince them they can't do without Lawrence Freeman, or Lawrence Freeman Produce.

Even the faithful support of his mother and sisters couldn't soften his father's blows. His father never laid a hand on him, but he still took Peter down. Lawrence Freeman could have found the time to go to San Francisco to see more of his son's games, but work was always his excuse, and his mother and sisters, trying to keep some semblance of peace in the Freeman family, enabled his father's excuses for his absences.

"All right!" Peter shouted out loud. His instinct to find the opening on the field kicked in, telling him to just shut up, get up off the bed, pee, get into his jogging suit—don't forget the elastic knee braces—and run 2 miles north on the beach, past the Cliff House to Lincoln Park. From Lincoln Park he could see the Golden Gate Bridge, its 746-foot towers majestically piercing the morning fog. That beautiful monument of man's achievement never ceased to inspire and encourage him. He often stayed there for a half-hour or more, looking at the Bridge, his jogging suit protecting him from the cold ocean breeze. Today, the Golden Gate Bridge would, as usual, give him the strength to do what he had to do.

Connie Satori—dark-blonde, pretty, pleasant, soft and lonely—stood on the deck for perhaps five minutes, watching her son Corey's vigil at the cliff. She didn't wonder what he was thinking, she didn't have to. Often she wished that she couldn't tell what he was thinking, preferring a mother's blissful ignorance that all was well with her tall, blonde, handsome, athletic, scholarly, 17-year-old son. But instead she had to accept the burden of awareness of her son's unfulfilled passion, a burning energy which was in need of being channeled.

What had always particularly amazed Connie about her son, though, was how effortlessly he seemed to restrain himself, to control whatever burgeoning energies he might have that his father and La Sangre—the two had become synonymous over the past 12 years—had imposed on Corey, the Pastor's son. While Connie had to work at repressing her continually rising irritation with Sal and La Sangre, Corey took it in stride, as if patiently plotting his exodus.

Exodus? Like maybe this weekend? Connie wondered what made her think that, and remembered she'd felt it this morning when Sal got out of bed before her. There was an urgency, an extra haste as he dressed for his morning walk down Highway 1.

Connie shook her head and turned her thoughts back to Corey, deciding whether or not to go out on the bluff and talk with him. He had never considered her an invader of his privacy, but now she wondered if their special communication might hinder rather than help him. No, she'll go to him. He probably was expecting her to do so anyway.

Connie carefully chose her opening line as she stepped down from the deck and walked out to join him. He didn't turn to acknowledge her presence, he didn't have to.

"The seagulls are louder than usual this morning," Corey said when she reached his right side.

"Yes, I noticed it too." As if in forewarning, they reminded her of the Alfred Hitchcock movie that had so terrified her as a child. She thought about mentioning it to Corey, but it would only be a stall for what she had to say. "It's a new life for you," she said instead, joining his gaze at the ocean. Corny, but true.

"It's about time, Mom."

She smiled ruefully. "I appreciate everything you've done, Corey."

"What I've done?" He turned to her, knowing what she meant, but needing to hear it.

"You know what I mean, all that you've put up with. Being home schooled, unable to join in school sports."

"I'm a great sprinter," he looked southward. "Up and down California State Route 1."

"I know." Corey hadn't gotten that talent from Connie or Sal. "But besides the home schooling, you didn't have the social advantages, making friends, meeting girls, dances, that kind of thing."

"Dancing?" Corey looked at her.

Connie smiled. "I always wanted to, at your age. But I was a wallflower."

"Wallflower?"

"Nobody asked me to dance." That wasn't exactly true. One boy did ask her. Just once.

"Oh." Corey turned back to the ocean. "Well, I'll get all that. Anyway Mom, don't sell your home-schooling short. Remember my high SAT scores. You did that."

"No, *you* did." Connie paused before deciding to proceed. "So, is it going to be Sacramento State, UC Berkeley, UCLA? They need a response soon." All three that Corey had applied to had accepted him.

"Mom, suppose," Corey hesitated, "well just suppose I went to Santa Rosa Junior College for the first two years, just to finish off the general ed requirements. Try out for the track team, maybe get a scholarship."

A flash of anger went through Connie as she grabbed his arm. "Absolutely not! Corey look at me! You're not staying here to take care of me, I'll be fine! You are *leaving* La Sangre!"

"Mom, it'll be cheaper. You and Dad don't have the money for a four-year college, you know that. With the church's salary?"

"Your father has money invested," she glanced at a few of the homes that they owned and rented out, not to mention the La Sangre businesses.

"Oh Mom, you told me yourself that those businesses don't make any money, and the rent he collects barely covers the mortgages. Besides, you know Dad wants me to go to Santa Rosa, that's why he's setting me up in the room over the La Sangre Garage, to give me some kind of 'freedom' while still having control over me."

Connie took a fast intake of breath and took her hand off Corey's arm. Rarely did they have to state the obvious to each other, usually such things remained unsaid between them. His statement surprised them both.

Corey softened his tone. "Mom, after junior college, he wants me to go to Bethany Bible College in Santa Cruz. As a pastor, he knows chances are good he'll be able to get a scholarship for that, at least for my junior and senior years."

"But Corey, is that what you want? Do you want to be a pastor? You should know how it is."

Yes, Corey knew how it was. He saw the hypocrisy, the smugness, the apparent inability for La Sangre's residents, except for maybe one or two, to think for themselves and instead to rely totally on the Pastor, his father, for their personal decisions. He could never be a part of that.

They both looked at the ocean for a minute while Connie carefully considered her next words. Such consideration wasn't usual between them, but she knew today was crucial. Maybe that's what she felt when she awoke this morning, something crucial about this weekend. "Don't worry about the money, Corey," she told him. "Besides, you've applied for a California State Scholarship. Given our income, or lack of it, I'm sure you'll get one. We'll hear soon."

"Maybe this weekend. In today's mail."

Connie started. "This weekend?"

Corey turned to her. "You feel it too Mom, I know you do. It's why I came out here this morning."

It was no use minimizing that connection they'd always had. Connie had given up on that years ago.

She sighed. "I felt it the minute I woke up. I think your father did too."

"I know he did."

That explained the seagulls' unusual behavior, although Connie wondered how much of that was some imaginative fear, a remnant of a frightened 12-year-old girl in a movie theater in Bakersfield. That, plus the Hitchcock film took place in Bodega Bay, just south of La Sangre. No, that was too simple. As she and Corey had agreed, there was something more to it.

They waited a moment to make sure they were through, but there was no more to say.

"I'm going to take my run," Corey announced the end of the conversation. He turned and walked towards the dirt road leading up to Highway 1.

Connie watched him walk off. He reminded her of a boy she used to know, the boy who had asked her to dance, who was also 17 at the time.

Corey knew his mother was watching him. Normally he would have turned and given her his usual "Everything's all right with me, Mom" smile, reassuring her, reminding her they were friends.

But for the first time he didn't turn around, and they both took note of it.

THREE

Peter Freeman parked his red, custom-striped four-wheel drive Ford F-250 pick-up outside O'Mahony's Sports Bar and Grill on Geary Street in San Francisco. During his run that morning, with the endorphin-high it always gave him, he'd come up with a plan: to live his life like running down field, one yard at a time. Yes, he had a phone call to make, that would be a touchdown, but in the meantime just concentrate on the first-and-ten. And the next first-and-ten was breakfast.

He locked his truck—he always did in San Francisco—walked to the curb and put coins in the meter and went inside.

"Pete!" the bartender hailed him as he entered O'Mahony's, unaware he'd just validated Peter's sense of self. Jeff O'Mahony, fat, bald, and outgoing, had the gift of validating everybody who entered his bar and grill.

"Jeff," Peter returned the greeting.

"Right here, sit right here bud," Jeff motioned to the stool closest to the barmaid station.

"We can talk better." Jeff was in his early 40s, a former high school football player and Forty-Niners fan who took Peter's frequency to his bar as an enormous blessing. He waited until Peter settled himself before saying more quietly, with the rough graciousness of a buddy, "Hey Pete, sorry about your old man."

"Yeah," Peter nodded, meeting Jeff's eyes. "Yeah, thanks."

"Pretty sudden, huh? I mean, he didn't have any kind of heart history, did he?"

"No, not at all. It just happened."

"Yeah, happens that way sometimes." Jeff shook his head. "Just 57 years old. Not that much older than I am." Peter noted that Jeff knew his father's age, and that it had somehow slipped through the Lawrence Freeman Produce PR machine.

"Well, I'll be happy to go that way myself," Jeff continued. "Coffee?" It was 10 AM, but O'Mahony's opened earlier than most sports bars, and it served breakfast. Even so, there was a group of enthusiastic drinkers at the table nearest the large-screen TV.

"Yeah, I need some coffee," Peter answered. "I'll order some breakfast in a bit."

"All right. Say Pete?" Jeff motioned discreetly to the busy table, with a waitress in attendance.

Peter followed Jeff's glance. Kristi. She nodded to the boys' order and then looked up and met Peter's eyes; hers and Peter's were two pair of blue eyes that had stayed locked-in for over three years.

Peter nodded to her and turned back to Jeff. "What's she doing here?"

Jeff raised his eyebrows and shrugged. "Just started last week. Needed a job, again."

It was no secret that Kristi had taken up with another Forty-Niner when she'd left Peter after the 1982 Superbowl win. Now here she was, waitressing again, back where they had originally met in 1979. She came up to the barmaid station and set down her tray of empty glasses.

"Hi Pete." She removed the empties from the tray and set them on the bar as Jeff set down Peter's mug of coffee. "Five regular draft, one dark," she told Jeff.

"Hi Kristi," Peter said, glancing at the getting-rowdy table. "I see the San Francisco Irish are out early."

Kristi followed his glance. "Oh yeah, they're getting primed for the fight this afternoon." She leaned in to Peter. "I'm so sorry about your Dad."

"Thanks babe," Peter said. He thought about commenting on the fact that she was back to waitressing, but thought better of it. Besides, he knew the reason why.

"Funny seeing you like this," Kristi said, as if reading Peter's mind. "This is where we met.

How long ago was that?"

"Just over five years." Peter could have nearly named the date.

"Five years! Where does the time go?"

They'd been together for the first three of
those years, friendly-then-intimate from the
very beginning. But also from the beginning
there was an unspoken contract between them
that their relationship basically consisted of all
the NFL trappings: the games, parties, awards
ceremonies, dinners in San Francisco's top restaurants, expensive vacations during the off-
season. He bought clothes for her. They both
took pleasure in going to I. Magnin where she'd
try on outfits for his approval and purchase.
With the perfect body, the perfect proportion
of breasts, waist, and hips, Kristi looked good
in anything. She was firm with just the right
amount of give to his touch. Her natural blonde
hair put all the bottle-blondes to shame, and her
blue eyes, like Peter's, never left his. "You know,
you always look right at me when we make love,"
she'd told him many times. "Where else would
I look?" was Peter's rather naive response. Her
laughter at his response told him that she'd had
more experience than he cared to know about.

Kristi had moved into his condo less than six
months into their relationship, but it was more
of a convenience than any strong need to con-
stantly be with each other, nor with any promise

of a future together. They both knew that, it was part of the contract. And the most important disclosure of that contract was that their love (if that was the word) wouldn't last without the NFL, not for five minutes. If they were placed on a desert island together, their blue eyes would have studied each other and wondered what to say. Peter tried to bring this up once but Kristi just laughed and said "Oh Pete, you *think* too much!"

And now, at the same age as he, she was still beautiful, still had the pleasing personality, but she was no longer a spring chicken. The early-twenties girls, always on the sidelines, had entered the game. Peter knew that's what necessitated her return to O'Mahony's.

Kristi's blue eyes stayed on Peter's during his thoughts, which took seconds but felt longer. Peter and Kristi knew they were, as before, in sync. Still, if either of them even considered it, they also knew there was no future between them. Their own futures were doubtful enough individually, let along together.

"Kristi," Peter broke their shared reverie, "I just want you to be happy."

She looked down, breaking eye contact. "Sure Pete." She chuckled. "Whatever *that* is."

"Hey, you tell me and we'll both know."

"*You* don't know? The Superbowl Champ?"

"Five regular, one dark," Jeff interrupted as

he set six glasses of beer on the bar. Kristi picked them up, two at a time, and placed them on her round, cork-lined service tray, creating new wet rings over the old dry ones.

Breakfast eaten, Peter studied his reflection in the mirror behind the bar. Okay, he'd gotten the first and ten, and was waiting for the next handoff.

Do it. Make the phone call.

"Say Pete," Jeff said while washing glasses. "Funny you should come in here this morning. Today's the three-year anniversary of my sobriety. Thanks to you."

"No Jeff," Peter looked at him evenly. "You would have done it without me. What amazes me is how you've maintained it while working here."

In unsolicited validation, a gale of raucous laughter exploded at the table of drinkers. Jeff glanced at them with a smile. "It's God's power, not mine, as we say in AA. Say Pete, are you going to stay around tor the fight? It starts in an hour. 3 PM Eastern time."

Peter didn't answer right away as he maintained his gaze at himself in the mirror. He envisioned an *Enquirer*-type headline: "Retired football player now spends all his time in a San Francisco bar," along with an altered photo. Of course, it hadn't come to that, but it wasn't unlike a few other retired players who, rather than go into insurance, real estate, or invest in a car dealership, found other ways to pass their time. Several took up golf, one he knew of was partying himself to death, another seemed to be gambling away his earnings, another was on his third, failing marriage, still another got into religion and spoke at various churches ("God's power, not mine"). Most were happily or unhappily married, with or without kids.

None of that interested Peter, like none of the permanent gigs his agent was offering him. And now LFP was waiting for his call. "No, I don't think so," Peter responded aloud both to Jeff's invitation and to his own thoughts. He pulled out his wallet to settle up.

The phone at the end of the bar rang and Jeff went to answer it. "Pete!" Jeff called to him, holding the receiver against his huge flaccid chest. "Phone."

Peter laid his cash on the bar. "If it's my agent, tell him I can't talk right now."

Jeff shook his head. "It's your Mom."

Peter snapped to alert and walked over to the phone.

"Mom, everything all right?"

"Hi Honey, yes, we're all right here. I left a message on your answering machine, but I wanted to make sure I caught you. I feel funny calling you there, but I know you eat breakfast there sometimes."

"That's fine Mom," Peter said. She didn't have to explain.

"Well, Barb and Diane went back to LA, Anne and Linda are staying with me for a while. We're thinking about going up to Lake Tahoe for a week, just to get out of the house. I don't want to deal with anything else right now."

"That's a good idea. Will you use the same house in Tahoe?"

"Yes, we checked, and it's available. Do you want to join us?"

"I don't know, maybe. I need to get out of San Francisco for a while. Why don't you leave a message on my answering machine with the phone number when you get there. I'll check my messages, okay?"

"Okay." His mother paused, and Peter waited. "Peter, this is hard to say, but...your father did love you...well, in his way he did."

"And just what 'way' was that?" Peter had an image of his father at one of the few Forty-Niner games he attended, wearing a Lawrence Freeman Produce cap and jacket. In fact, he never wore a Forty-Niner cap, anywhere.

"I don't know," she sighed. "He was easier on the girls, but with you...it was different, because you were a boy, a young man." She paused. "I guess we should have talked about it before, but...Peter, he dealt with you like the men he's, he *was*, in business with, with the city, the county, the state, his rivals and competitors."

His competitor. Peter froze. That's what he was. He'd never thought about it before, not consciously, but that's what he was to his father.

"Peter?"

"You...you never said that before."

"Oh Peter, how could I? I was trying so hard just to keep some kind of...peace. If we'd had all girls it would have been different, but you were his only son."

It did make sense, but it didn't make it any easier. "Mom, thanks for telling me that, but don't sweat it, okay? I just need some time. Maybe I'll drive up the coast, I need to think. We can talk about it at Tahoe, okay?"

"Okay Peter. You be careful, all right?"

"Okay."

"I'll call you when we get set up at Lake Tahoe. I love you Peter. "

"I love you Mom."

FOUR

S al walked along the path that wound through
the cluster of homes until he arrived at the
small cottage on the south end of the bluff. It
was the Owens' summer home, and they weren't
really a part of La Sangre. At Sal's arrival and
mighty efforts twelve years ago to bring the
small community together under the La Sangre
Christian Church, people had either fallen into
the fold, or sold their homes (at a tidy California-
equity profit) and moved out.

But the Owens had done neither, spending their summers in quiet solitude, appreciat-
ing but otherwise ignoring the pleasant Sunday
morning church bells. They were gracious and
friendly when they visited the La Sangre Grocery
and General Stores, but mostly they made their
purchases and did their eating out in Santa
Rosa. From Labor Day to Father's Day they went
home to Redding and rented out the cottage;
there was never a shortage of potential and reliable renters for an oceanside home, even during
the winter. Nurse Lillian Walker, in addition to

running the General Store and Post Office, collected the rent and served as the Owens' rental manager for a decent fee.

The Owens' tenant this time was a Jessie Malana, and her connection with the Owens was vague, even mysterious. They apparently knew her in Redding, and she must have had the proper references as the Owens approved of her, and apparently she'd passed the credit check they made. Jessie drove an expensive-looking black sports car, fast and loud, which could always be heard approaching town from the north, if she had gone in to Santa Rosa, or from the south, if she'd gone to San Francisco. Where did she get the money for such a car? Certainly not from the waitressing job she'd talked Sal into giving her at the La Sangre Saloon. She took to the job easily. Had she been a waitress before? If not, what had she done?

Sal had pumped both Lillian and Jessie herself for details, but the responses from both women were vague. Lillian honestly knew very little, other than that the Owens were satisfied with Jessie's monthly rent payments and Lillian's reports on Jessie as a responsible tenant. But Jessie herself had a knack—indeed a great talent—for deflection. It was subtle and effective. Sal found himself extremely frustrated when he tried to get answers from Jessie, and even when he raised his voice, something he used when all else failed, Sal was unable to get past her shield. So he figured he'd just give it some time and pray about the situation, asking the Lord to give him the strength to break her down.

From the start, Jessie never missed church, both the Sunday morning and evening services, nor the Ladies' Tuesday Night Prayer Group, and the Wednesday Night Bible Study. But even the other ladies, again at Sal's prompting, couldn't get to really know Jessie, other than to say she was very pretty and she obviously loves the Lord, praying and studying her Bible and asking questions and listening. She even sings in their small choir. What else was necessary to prove she was indeed saved?

But Satan is subtle, Sal reminded himself. He wondered if the warning he'd had this morning was about Jessie; but no, it was something else, something coming *into* La Sangre, not something that was already here. So Sal would just bide his time with Jessie. In the meantime, a Satanic sabotage after twelve years of his being in La Sangre was not only possible, but even likely by this time. Satan could indeed attack and attempt to destroy La Sangre, this spiritual haven that Sal had prayed and fought for to build and maintain. Twelve years of God's peace couldn't convince him to drop his caution with anyone. Not with the Owens, not with anyone.

And now this girl...this Jessie...

She walked out onto the porch just as Sal approached the gate to the Owens' small yard, as if she had been alerted to his visit, perhaps even knowing what he was thinking. She remained on the porch, standing casually, waiting. She was a nondescript mid- to late-thirties, very fair, with short wispy blonde hair, and light skin. Her features were fine, her body small-framed and compact, with her bra-less tank top and too-short shorts revealing small breasts and very nice legs. Like one of those Greek statues, Sal thought. Very feminine, not at all hard and unyielding like women's bodies today with overly firm breasts, often manufactured, and flat hard stomachs and muscled legs.

Sal realized he had been thinking about this, aware of it more and more lately, even in church while he preached. But summer had begun, the Owens were arriving, and she was leaving. That was all that mattered.

"Good morning Pastor," Jessie finally said, her eyes not straying from his strong gaze, a gaze that never frightened her. She always met his challenge.

"Jessie," he nodded in return, once again irritated at his lack of control where she was concerned. If Doyle was at one end of the scale of his control, Jessie was at the other end. She was also at the other end of the scale from Doyle's lack of intelligence; Jessie had an intelligence as powerful as her sexuality. And she was so damned *observant.*

And now here she was, standing on the porch, observing him and obviously enjoying the advantage of the three-step height she had over Sal. She waited placidly to hear the reason for his visit. Asking him "What can I do for you Pastor?" would make it too easy for him, something she never did. He always had to make the first move, and she could build her defense from there.

"I was wondering" Sal began, deciding to dispense with any pleasantries since by this time it no longer mattered, "have you heard from the Owens yet?"

She paused a moment, the way he did with Doyle, he realized. "A letter came in yesterday," she said plainly. "They'll be here this Monday, as planned."

"Did they say anything else?"

"About what?" It was Strike One against him, but her flat tone belied it.

Sal closed his eyes briefly in retaliation. "Are there any supplies," he kept his voice level, "they would like me to order for them, anything special they want done for their arrival?"

"I've taken care of everything."

"They didn't say anything in particular?"

Jessie thought about delivering another

"About what?" but she didn't. It was too easy and besides, she was certain she'd strike him out, as always. "They did say they're bringing Mrs. Owen's aunt with them."

"Her aunt? Where is she from?"

"They didn't say anything about her."

"Will she be staying the whole summer?"

"They didn't say anything about her," Jessie repeated. Strike Two.

"Is she a Christian?" And Sal caught himself too late.

Jessie smiled at the mockery of his inquisition. Sal closed his eyes again in an effort to let Jessie think that he was irritated with her, rather than with his own inadequacy around her. He opened his eyes again and she was still looking at him, not defiantly, just quietly and easily. Damn this girl!

Jessie strategically waited for Sal to speak. Strike Three coming up.

"Never mind," Sal struggled to keep his voice level. "I've asked Martha to help the other women get ready for the Father's Day picnic. Can you and Jeremiah hold down the Saloon by yourself after lunch?" Jeremiah was the cook.

"We won't have a problem."

"Just send for Martha if it gets particularly busy."

Jessie nodded.

"And what about Corey's graduation cake?

Connie and I thought we'd cut it there at the Saloon, when we come over for lunch today."

"I was just going to drive into Santa Rosa to pick it up. I'll be back in time to join Martha during the lunch rush."

Against his will, Sal glanced down at her skimpy attire, wondering if she was going to drive to the Santa Rosa Bakery dressed like that, a whorey representation of La Sangre. A rush of heat went through him as he pictured her walking into the bakery, her breasts and legs shimmering....

Jessie smiled at his review of her body. Strike Three, you're out. *Pastor* Satori.

Sal's unexpected desire for her turned into fury. He pressed his lips together before speaking. "What are you going to do?"

"I just told you. I'm going to drive to Santa Rosa." Strike Four, if there was such a thing, but the inning was over, top of the ninth. The game would be over soon, by Father's Day.

"No!" Sal raised his voice. "I mean what are you going to do when the Owens return? Where will you go?"

"South," she said firmly. Her tone was unmistakable: it's none of your business.

Sal automatically glared at Jessie, the first time he'd done so with her. His patented glares were designed to wither and intimidate. It worked for everyone else in La Sangre when necessary for what he deemed discipline. But he knew, too late, it wouldn't work on Jessie. So he quickly switched to his other offensive, one he had used with Jessie many times, his charming Pastor's smile, a little too wide and showing too many teeth.

For the first time since her arrival, Jessie returned his smile with a supercilious one that bordered on laughter. Sal turned on his heel and walked away.

Damn her! Damn her to hell! Jessie was the only person in La Sangre around whom Sal felt weak and out of control. And impotent.

FIVE

Shortly after 11 AM Peter was driving north across the Golden Gate Bridge, hoping again that its looming orange towers, the graceful arc of its suspension, the powerful Pacific Ocean to the west, and the approaching lush green hills of Marin County would lift his spirits. Somehow, unusually, none of it had done so when he had watched it from Lincoln Park during his run. So in O'Mahony's Peter determined his next first-and-ten was to drive across the Bridge and look at it from the other side. From there, he could keep driving north, and the treasures of Northern California could offer him a new life. He might keep driving as far north up US 101 as Fortuna maybe, or Eureka. Maybe he could buy some land up there, build a house in the redwoods, maybe even use redwoods to build it. He would have his home on the beach in San Francisco and his cabin in the redwoods. He had the money to do it. He wouldn't take a job, not with LFP nor anyone else, and he wouldn't have to be ashamed about not having a job. He'd earned his financial freedom. He could just relax and enjoy it.

If he could relax and enjoy it. Therein lay a second rub, following the first rub he'd felt when he woke up this morning, about following his heart. He didn't know where his heart was. And yes, a cabin in the redwoods was financially doable, but it was a fantasy. How could he relax and enjoy a fantasy? And wouldn't he just be hiding?

At the north end of the Bridge Peter exited to the viewing area on the east side of 101. He'll park for a while. Maybe the view of downtown San Francisco and the sound of the ocean, in addition to the Bridge, will help. He parked his truck facing the city and got out. He leaned against the hood. The fog had long lifted, but the beauty of San Francisco and all that it had meant to him, his career, the freedom it had brought, was gone. He looked at the skyline, bright and distinct, with the Bay Bridge, Coit Tower, and the Transamerica Pyramid marking themselves. Somehow San Francisco was no longer his, at least not right now. Had he lost it for good?

He looked at the Golden Gate Bridge, but like earlier this morning, the Bridge made it clear that it had its own confidence and manhood that Peter couldn't latch onto. Just like he could no longer latch onto the San Francisco Forty-Niners. Isn't that why Kristi had left him?

After he retired, she was left with just Peter Freeman, period. And that's all that Peter was left with now: just himself.

He looked down at the San Francisco Bay and followed a freighter that was heading west under the Bridge towards the Pacific Ocean. If only he could hop off the Bridge, land safely on the freighter, and head off into the Pacific. Would that be following his heart? No. On that freighter he'd still be hiding. Another fantasy. Was that all he had now, fantasies? And what about jumping from the Bridge onto the freighter? Was that some kind of suicidal fantasy?

Where is the opening? That opening he always managed to find on the gridiron? It had always appeared before. Now instead of an opening, there was an abyss.

Peter, remember what you decided this morning, about taking one yard at a time. Think short term, starting with just this weekend. You can't stay in San Francisco this weekend, but driving to Lake Tahoe to join your Mom and sisters wouldn't do it either; they'd just be talking about your father and you can't do that, at least not now.

Peter took a few deep breaths, and after fifteen minutes of half-looking at the city, the Bridge, the bay and the ocean, he got back into his truck. He couldn't see the next yard, let alone the next first-and-ten.

He was down. Whistle blown. The abyss.

He reached for the ignition and started the engine, just for something to do. But he didn't know where he was going, other than an undefined northerly direction. That was all he had.

He gripped the steering wheel fiercely. "What in God's name am I going to do!" he screamed out loud.

A rap on the driver's window shook him. A man in his 40s was standing there: taller than Peter, maybe six-five, seemingly solid, with shoulder-length reddish-blonde hair and full beard. He wore a red-plaid jacket, like what a lumberjack might wear. He had a questioning look on his rugged, handsome face.

Peter lowered the window.

"Hey man," the stranger asked, "are you all right?" He must have been standing there long enough to hear Peter scream.

Peter nodded, embarrassed, then decided it didn't matter. "Yeah, I'm all right. I think."

"I saw you exit from the Bridge. You heading north?"

Peter nodded. *That* much he knew. That was all he knew.

"Do you mind...can you give me a lift? I'm going up to Eureka."

The hitchhiker waited, while Peter looked at him. Eureka, up by the California/Oregon border.

"I've got my dog here," the hitchhiker looked down. Peter followed his glance to an Irish Setter standing next to him, eager and obedient, his coat the same reddish-blonde hue as the hitchhiker. "I saw you had a pickup. That's why I asked you. He's fine to ride in the back."

Without responding Peter opened the driver door as the hitchhiker stepped back, and walked to the tailgate and lowered it. The hitchhiker and the dog followed him, the hitchhiker said "Barney, up," and the dog jumped into the back without questioning it. The hitchhiker threw in his backpack, Peter shut the gate and walked to the driver door while the hitchhiker went to the passenger door.

Engine still running, Peter gripped the steering wheel again but did nothing else.

The hitchhiker settled himself in the passenger seat and fastened his seat belt. He turned to Peter, studying him. "Hey man, are you sure you're all right?"

Peter tried to give an automatic nod, but couldn't. He wanted to answer "No," but was afraid to. It would be giving in, like jumping off the Golden Gate Bridge and hitting the freighter, or hitting the freezing cold water.

"So how far are you going?" the hitchhiker asked.

Peter looked at him. "I don't know," was all he could manage.

"Well, as far north as you can get me is fine." He held out his hand. "I'm Jay. Jay Carpenter."

"Pete Freeman." They shook hands.

"I thought I recognized you. Hey man, you played a great Superbowl two years ago."

Peter looked away, back at the Bridge. "You think so?"

"Yes, I do."

Peter turned back to him. "Thanks. I needed that."

The hitchhiker—Jay, Peter noted—nodded simply. Peter returned the nod as he put the truck into gear, backed out of the parking space, and headed to the entrance of northbound US 101.

They rode in a warm, strangely comfortable silence for several minutes until they approached the turnoff for Northbound California State Route 1, at Mill Valley.

"Mind if I take the coast route?" Peter asked. "I could use it."

"As long as it's north, I'm good."

After a few more minutes, Peter began to speak suddenly, unexpectedly. "Did you ever get the feeling that you—or that your life—was stuck in halftime?"

Jay gave an easy smile. "Sure I have. Why do you think I'm doing this? On the road." He pointed a thumb behind him, to his dog, his backpack, and the receding road. "I'm not going back, not going to start the second half, until I know I can do it right."

"Do it right," Peter repeated. "How do you know when you're doing it right?"

"You just know," Jay said firmly. "You know because you know. Like all those great running plays you made with the Niners. You didn't have to *think* about it, did you?"

Peter shook his head. "As soon as the ball was handed off or lateraled to me, I just took off."

"You just *did* it," Jay agreed, "like Moses parting the Red Sea."

Peter smiled at the reference. An NFL fan.

"I also liked how," Jay continued, "when you scored a touchdown, you didn't throw the ball down or dance a jig."

"Yeah," Peter agreed, "that's show-biz stuff. I was never into that. I just held the ball up to show I had possession."

Jay paused thoughtfully for a moment. "You know, back at the Bridge, when I said that you played a great Superbowl Game, you seemed surprised, like you didn't believe it. I'm sure that people tell you that all the time. The press especially."

"Yeah but..." Peter half-turned to Jay, keeping his left eye on the road. "I guess it's just that..." he stopped talking and turned back fully to the road, the comforting, reliable road that was now California State Route 1 and would lead him into Mill Valley, through the Muir Woods, and then to the Pacific Ocean.

"I like the road," Peter said instead.

"Me too. Open and free. With a destination."

"That's the only thing I don't have," Peter replied.

"You don't have a destination?"

Peter didn't know this guy who had jumped into his truck, but he needed to talk to him like he hadn't talked to anybody in a long time. "See, my Dad died a week ago, and I'm trying to figure it out. He never really gave me an unqualified compliment on my playing. There was always some little thing he'd throw in that would make me doubt my ability. It's like everything I did, everything I felt I was, wasn't all there. I mean, I was no O.J. Simpson, and Ricky Patton and Earl Cooper got more yardage and outscored me, but I played good games, made good yardage, never fumbled, scored points, and helped win Superbowl Sixteen. And yet without my Dad's approval, there was always something missing."

Jay smiled at the road ahead of them. "Yeah, welcome to the 'You'll-Never-Be-Good-Enough Club.' That's why I quit the police force."

"You were a cop?" Peter glanced at Jay's long hair and beard.

"Undercover. L.A.P.D., almost twenty years."

"You didn't like it?"

"Oh I loved the work, and didn't even mind all the bureaucratic stuff, the paperwork, court appearances. But while I was out there trying to enforce law and order, I had to look at the things that people...that we do to each other, to ourselves. And no matter how hard I worked, it wasn't getting better. I felt like an accountant with his in-basket overflowing, and the faster I worked, it didn't diminish the pile, it just kept increasing. And in my in-basket were assaults, rapes, murders...."

"So," Peter ventured, "you burned out?"

"Cracked up," Jay answered plainly. "Had a nervous breakdown. Right there on Sunset Boulevard while I was busting a couple of hookers. These two girls were maybe sixteen years old, and all of a sudden I found myself seeing them as little girls, riding their tricycles, playing dolls, crying because their balloons popped or they dropped their snow cones on the ground. As little girls they were still innocent, hopeful, still dreaming and believing, because they had their whole lives ahead of them. But somehow they became broken, and couldn't fix themselves."

Jay stopped talking while Peter waited.

"That was the part that did me in," Jay continued, still looking at the road that was now winding into the green darkness of Muir Woods, "that they couldn't fix themselves. But I couldn't fix them either. As a cop I was useless and impotent." He stopped again.

Jay's simple words were hitting Peter in the gut. "What did you do?" Peter finally asked him. "Did you bust them?"

Jay shook his head. "No, I couldn't do it. Not any more. I just walked away from them, down Sunset Boulevard. My unmarked car was parked on a side street, but I just kept on walking, west on Sunset all the way through Hollywood, Beverly Hills, Bel Air, Pacific Palisades, twenty miles to the Pacific Ocean. The only reason I stopped at the beach was because I couldn't walk on the water. When I realized I couldn't walk on water I sat down in the sand and cried." He paused, remembering and reliving it. "They found me the next morning."

Peter waited to make sure the story was over. Sad, even tragic, but he could see that it was a peaceful acceptance for Jay. It was history.

"When did this happen?" Peter asked.

"Last January."

"Last January," Peter repeated thoughtfully. That was when he'd begun to realize that he didn't know what he was going to do. That was when the doubts and questions started piling up on the in-box, as Jay had said. Then his father's death crashed down on the in-box, cracking it and scattering the papers. And now Lawrence Freeman Produce was waiting for a phone call.

"They transferred me to desk work," Jay

continued, "after I'd gotten out of the hospital, gone through therapy, and recovered. But I wasn't into it. I was just going through the motions, working with an actual in-box this time, doing the work, collecting a paycheck, and going home. There was no woman in my life, no one to do it for. I'm divorced—the police work had done that—no kids. So I quit. I had some money saved up. I got Barney," he motioned back to his dog, "short for Barnabas, and decided to hitch hike up the coast, into Canada."

"You'd mentioned Eureka."

"There's someone there I'm going to visit, also a former cop. We've kept in touch."

Peter thought about it. In his truck he always carried a Forty-Niners overnight bag with deodorant, razor and shaving cream, a change of socks and underwear. He had a credit card, he could buy anything else he needed.

"I can get you to Eureka," Peter decided. "We'll get there late this evening. Well, maybe not, since we're taking the coast route."

"Sounds great either way," Jay grinned and leaned back in the seat.

"Except do me a favor, will you?"

"Name it."

"Let's not talk about the Forty-Niners. In fact no football talk at all. All right?"

Jay broke into a hearty laugh. "Sure, Peter."

Peter noted that Jay had called him "Peter"

instead of the usual "Pete," but it didn't matter. Route 1 was catching intermittent rays of sunshine beaming through openings in the redwood canopy of John Muir Woods. In a half hour they'd be at the Pacific Ocean.

70 miles to the north, La Sangre was waiting for them.

SIX

Business at the La Sangre General Store and Post Office was unusually light for a Saturday morning, just a few locals and no tourists. At 11:30 AM Lillian Walker went outside to the wooden walkway (complete with hitching rails, she always smirked at them) that ran the two-block length of La Sangre. Across the road and to the north, past the Saloon, Doyle Seeno was putting gas into a tourist's car, a small economy model. Lillian's smirk at the hitching rails remained as she wondered how long the Pastor would hold onto his "Last-Chance-Gas" mentality. It was as silly as the hitching rails, the wooden walkway, and the Western false fronts of all five buildings.

Lillian remembered growing up in La Sangre in the 1940s and 50s, when indeed the gas pumps were a welcome sight for the coast drivers, and indeed a few locals had horses. As a little girl she would walk up from her home on the bluff and sit on the bench in front of the gas station, observing the travelers as they'd get out to stretch and use the rest room. Sometimes they'd browse in the Antique Store, or go into the Saloon for a drink and something to eat, or they'd cross the road to the General Store or Grocery Store. Lillian would study their cars, their shiny colors adorned with chrome, and fantasize about sneaking into one of them and hiding on the floor in the back seat, waiting until the owners returned and drove off with her as a stowaway. She always chose the cars that were heading north. She fantasized that she would wait until they got up into Oregon or Washington, before she'd make her escape.

Significantly, Lillian's fantasy didn't include sneaking south as an option, that was of no interest to her. Her parents had taken her to San Francisco on a few occasions, to downtown Market Street to window shop, or to the Sutro Baths to peer through the big windows at the salt-water bathers. They'd stroll the midway of Playland-At-The-Beach amusement park near Sutro's, where her father would buy her a cotton candy, but he couldn't put her on the rides. Paying for the gas for the borrowed car and the one-dollar round trip toll over the Golden Gate Bridge was all they could afford. But that was fine with Lillian, she enjoyed the beauty of San Francisco and the cotton candy. Besides, it was North that really called her.

Lillian sighed at the wistful memory and

crossed her arms over her ruffled, floor-length Gay-90s style dress that the Pastor insisted she wear to add flavor to the General Store. That was one of the Pastor's demands she had no problem with. It actually improved what she knew was an ill-defined figure to go along with her mousy brown hair, thin lips, an almost beak-like nose, and probing brown, bespectacled eyes.

So this morning she watched Doyle check the oil and water in a small blue car, obviously relishing his job and his "position" in the town. ("None of this self-serve jazz," he'd tell anyone who would listen. "In La Sangre, we offer full service to the motorist!") Yes, he was the model La Sangre citizen, Lillian thought with her usual disdain.

Fortunately Lillian never have to contend with Doyle trying to court her, although they were the same age. Poor Doyle saw Lillian as a woman, and human, and he was still waiting, and praying, for his pristine goddess to be delivered out of the sky, probably riding a white-winged horse and escorted by angels. "The wife that God has promised me will be as fine a woman as Connie Satori," Doyle had once confided to Lillian. Of course, it was only Connie's position as the Pastor's wife that made Doyle admire her. Caught up in his fantasy, he was incapable of seeing Connie as the earthy and very real woman that Lillian knew she was.

And Lillian, Connie is prettier than you, isn't she? Wouldn't any man, including Doyle, prefer her?

Stop it! Lillian scolded herself. She had long admired Connie, envying her soft personality, her warm full figure and gently smiling eyes to her own somber appearance and manner. She had so much wanted to be Connie's friend, but outside of church and its activities, a one-on-one friendship with her proved impossible. And it hurt Lillian because she knew that it *was* possible. Connie needed a friend as much as Lillian did, but the Pastor's ever-looming presence was too strong, and he wouldn't be able to control the bond, the understanding, the shared secrets between two women.

What hurt even more was that Connie seemed to accept the situation, although Lillian was sure that deep down, Connie didn't want to be under her husband's iron thumb. Was she just used to it after 17 years of marriage? Or was she just so numb to it that it never occurred to her that her own thoughts, feelings, and needs were not being acknowledged, let alone met? Had Connie resigned herself to her husband's complete control of her own humanity?

Lillian shook her head in an attempt to once again rid herself of those 12-year-old nagging questions. Why couldn't she just forget it and let it be?

Well for that matter, Lillian, why can't *you* just forget this town and leave? Why can't you just leave La Sangre? Just take off and leave! You did it before, remember?

As if in confirmation of that, the small blue car pulled away from the gas station. Lillian watched it drive north, losing itself around a bend in the green coastal hills.

"Good morning Nurse Walker!" Doyle's overloud greeting drowned out her wistful, and disturbed, thoughts. He always called her Nurse Walker, reveling in the security of her title and position as he did in his own and the Pastor's and in everything else in this bubble-topped town. She wondered what Doyle's title might be, if he had one. Gas Jockey? He considered himself a mechanic. That was a laugh. Lillian would never let him touch her car...if she had one.

"Good morning Doyle," she returned, not disguising her sudden boredom. She was better off with her disquieting thoughts than with him.

"Nice day, ain't it?" Doyle went on, incapable of reading Lillian's bored response.

Isn't it, Doyle, she thought angrily. Not *ain't* it, *isn't* it! She studied him disparagingly before turning around and walking inside the General Store, perversely enjoying what must have been his surprised reaction at her rejection. Once inside she sat down behind the counter, feeling the emptiness of the quaintly contrived store around her. The canned goods and specialty candies, the quilts and pot holders made with loving care by the local women, further fueled her anger.

What was wrong? Why had Doyle set her off like that? Why did she feel like picking up a jar of La Sangre Homemade Jam and throwing it against the wall?

Because Lillian, you're wondering why can't you just leave La Sangre.

Oh yes, *that* question again. It seemed to be surfacing more and more lately, and particularly this Saturday morning. That nagging, persistent question. Why she had returned to La Sangre after being gone for 16 years she understood well enough. But why was she staying?

You're forty-eight years old, Lillian Walker. It's not too late. Don't retire from life. Keep going. You've still got time. You're in the Nurse's Registry, you can get a job anywhere. The value of your oceanside cottage has tripled, probably quadrupled, in value over the last 48 years. You could be what's called a "California Equity Emigrant." Sell and move somewhere.

But where to, Lillian?

"All right!" she raised her voice in the empty store. "I'll think about it after Father's Day. After this weekend is over!"

Suddenly the weekend became animated and horrible, like some indomitable monster from the south, coming to get her. And not just her, it was coming from the south to take over La Sangre. And once it was here, it would be too late for her, or anyone, to escape.

Peter and Jay stood on a turnout overlooking the Pacific Ocean. Peter felt good, even, and inexplicably, happy. He turned and looked at Jay, who was evidently in his own peaceful thoughts. It was strange: Peter never had a shortage of buddies before, he was always surrounded by supportive team members, hero-worshipers, followers. But this guy was different, solid and real, probably the most real person Peter had met in his life. And per his promise, Jay had never brought up football.

"Barney!" Jay called to his dog, who was barking at seagulls that hovered just beyond the edge of the cliff. Immediately the Setter responded with a jerk of his head towards Jay. "Watch that cliff!" Jay warned him. It would be easy for Barney to steal under the guard rail and go after the birds. Barney turned back to the elusive birds with a final I'll-get-you-later bark, and ran back to Jay and Peter.

"He's a good dog," Peter said as Barney settled himself between the two of them and looked up adoringly at Jay.

"Yeah, Barney's all right," Jay said. He reached down and squeezed his right ear. "I think more than anything else, more than the shrinks at the hospital, Barney helped me get it together again." He turned to Peter. "Dogs are like perfect people, you know? They love and trust, with no questions, no strings attached. They forgive and forget. Somehow they're able to absorb all of our problems and then release them with some healthy barks, and chasing birds."

"Chasing birds," Peter repeated thoughtfully. "They usually don't catch them, but they sure don't stop chasing after them." He turned to Jay in sudden realization. "This morning, I said I was stuck in halftime, but now, all of a sudden, it feels like the second half has started."

"And you're ready?"

"Put me in coach."

Jay didn't smile, instead frowned and nodded, then turned to his right and looked north up the coast.

"What's the matter?" Peter sensed Jay's sudden concern.

"So you're ready to play again?" Jay asked, avoiding Peter's observation.

"Yeah, but I want to make sure I don't fumble this time, not like I did in the first half."

"I never saw you fumble a ball."

"Well, figuratively."

"Figuratively? Like how?" Jay turned to the ocean and waited for Peter to answer the question.

"I don't think...."

Peter considered and Jay waited.

"I don't think I ever really loved anyone," Peter finally said. "There were women, and I even lived with one for three years." Peter realized with surprise that he suddenly couldn't remember her name. Oh yeah, Kristi. That was a long time ago. "There were women I could have married, beautiful, kind, do anything for me, willing to be a 'wife' without being politically correct about it. But I didn't know why I *should* marry them, other than the fact that it was what I was supposed to do as a man past 30. My Dad wanted a grandson." Peter sighed. "Yeah, it's what was expected of me, to have a trophy wife who makes a good appearance and decorates the house and will follow me to all the games and sit there with the other trophy wives. Just another trophy to go along with the Superbowl one. But Kristi—the girl I lived with—always did that stuff anyway, so it didn't really make a difference." He turned to Jay. "Am I making sense?"

Jay nodded, still watching the ocean. "Keep going."

"The only reason to get married, the only thing I knew I wanted, was a kid. A son. Not a grandson for my Dad, a son for me. I think that's what I've missed or needed more than anything else. But now, I'm not so sure that even *that's* what I wanted."

"Why do you say that?" Jay didn't move, just kept his eye on the ocean.

"Because..." Peter wrinkled his forehead, following Jay's surveillance of the sea. The truth was materializing, almost tangible in front of him, painful yet positive. "Because...I guess it's not that I wanted a son so much, but what I wanted was to somehow recreate myself, make a perfect and unblemished me, that I could love and accept."

Silence.

"Yes?" Jay encouraged Peter.

"I guess," Peter went on, "it would have been worse if I did have a son, because then I probably would have..." He stopped and felt the final pierce of truth go through him. "Jesus," he widened his eyes and turned to Jay. "I would have tried to create a new me, a perfect me, because I couldn't love and accept the old me. I would have done the same thing to my boy that my father did to me. I would have laid my expectations onto him. I would have been demanding instead of accepting. I wouldn't have set him free!"

"Corey!" Sal called up the stairs. "Letter for you!" He turned to Connie, who stood in the kitchen doorway watching. "It's from Bethany Bible College," he told her.

Connie nodded faintly and listened to Corey's pounding steps down the stairs, hating for that anticipatory excitement to be crushed.

"Who's it from?" Corey asked when he got down.

Sal handed him the envelope with a meaningful look. As if he were serving a summons, Connie thought.

"Oh," Corey muttered when he saw the return address, "Bethany. Well..." He looked at his mother, opened the envelope, and frowned at the letter.

"Well?" his father asked.

Corey hesitated. "They've offered me a four year scholarship." Not just the two years that Sal had requested. Four years.

"Well congratulations Son!" Sal held out his hand. "We weren't expecting that, were we? Four years! Praise the Lord!"

"Yeah, thanks," Corey shook his hand, not looking at him.

"That's wonderful Corey," Connie said, feeling ridiculous.

"That gives us two things to celebrate today," Sal said. "Your graduation, and your scholarship to Bethany Bible College." He looked at his watch. "Say, why don't we go over to the Saloon now and have lunch?"

Go to the "saloon" and have lunch? Connie mused. Does everything sound ridiculous today, or has it always?

"Fine," Corey nodded. He folded the letter and began to stuff it back into the envelope.

"Don't wrinkle it," Sal said. "You might want to frame it."

SEVEN

For the third time that morning, Lillian walked out of the General Store, stood on the wooden walkway, and looked south down Highway 1, in anticipation of what she knew was coming into La Sangre. Yes, anticipation, not the fear that she'd felt earlier. Anticipation and even excitement. She was still a woman, she happily remembered, and still had a thoroughly feminine intuition, something that she thought she'd lost along with her sexuality. Intuition and sexuality were undesirable traits in La Sangre, things to be buried under a mindless duty to serve God, all according to the Pastor. But now she could only hope—and yes pray—for the promise of a reawakening. Maybe that was why Doyle had set her off this morning. His Hail Virgin Lillian greeting this morning had offended the too-long-dead woman inside her.

Lillian was jolted out of her—were they fancies? no, *expectations*—by the deep roar of a high-powered sports car driving into town. Was this it? No, it was coming from the north, not the south. She watched as Jessie's black sports car executed a fast, smooth U-turn and came to a screeching halt in front of the Saloon. The maneuver displayed an obvious pleasure between Jessie and her vehicle, as a man might have with his. Lillian smiled. Jessie had spirit. She still didn't know anything about Jessie, other than she was from Redding and that's where she'd met the Owens. As a nurse, Lillian was usually adept at getting into people, but she got nowhere with Jessie. Jessie's comments and insights during Bible studies were very general, never specific to herself. After a while, Lillian gave up trying to get to know Jessie, as she had with Connie.

Lillian watched as Jessie, in her waitress uniform, deftly got out of the sports car (Lillian would have had a problem with her long legs) and made a sensuous stretch to the floor of the passenger seat, pulling out a square pink bakery box. There's one other person, besides herself, Lillian felt with kinship, who hadn't buried herself in this town. Wanting to...no, needing to talk to Jessie, Lillian crossed the road.

"Can I give you a hand?" Lillian asked her.

"What the hell would I do with three hands?" Jessie quipped. Her careless rough language brought a dry smile to Lillian. She knew the remark wasn't meant offensively; better, she knew that Lillian was the only one in town Jessie would make that kind of remark to. If the other La Sangre ladies heard her say "what the hell?" Oh my.

"It looks like that cake survived the rough ride," Lillian remarked in a rougher tone than she normally used. Whatever it was that Jessie had, it was contagious.

"Oh, it did plenty of slipping and sliding down there," Jessie smirked. "In fact, I think I clocked my best time on that windy road from Santa Rosa. I may have to serve this graduation cake scrambled. Get the door for me, will you?"

Lillian stepped up onto the walkway and opened the door to the Saloon. Inside, Martha was easily handling the few locals, as well as a middle-aged out-of-town couple. Jessie motioned to the couple when she went through the door. "Where'd *they* come from?" she asked Lillian in a low voice.

"From the north, about a half-hour ago."

"Oh," Jessie responded without interest.

"Why, are you expecting someone?"

After a hesitation, Jessie gave a firm "No."

"What time are you leaving tomorrow?" Lillian was enjoying their exchange; it was far more casual than any they'd had before.

"After church. Maybe after the picnic." Jessie set the box on the counter. "Well, let's see what the damage is." She cut the scotch-taped flaps with her strong fingernails and opened it.

The cake had chocolate icing, white trim, and a tiny, black, plastic graduation cap, with "Congratulations Corey" written in white. But the cake had indeed slid on its cardboard bottom, crushing one side and smearing frosting against the inside of the box.

"That's too bad," Lillian commented. The sense of joviality with Jessie was suddenly gone. She found herself sickened by the sight of the damaged cake.

"Well, we all have to go some time, don't we?" Jessie declared darkly.

Lillian murmured a talk-to-you-later and fled back across the road to the General Store. Just two minutes ago she had wanted to talk to Jessie, out of a need for camaraderie, to bond with someone who might understand what she was feeling. Now, she never wanted to talk to, or see, Jessie again.

When they passed the La Sangre City Limits sign and Peter saw the town, he impulsively turned right and pulled in front of the La Sangre Saloon. "Look at this place!" he exclaimed to Jay.

Peter had loved old western and mining ghost towns as a kid, since the first time his father had taken him to see the remnants of Freeman Junction, east of Bakersfield. Played out by the 1950s, the town was deserted by 1976, and by 1984, all remnants of the town had been picked dry by antique collectors and scavengers. "Do you know who this town is named after?" his father had asked him. "After you Daddy?" "No son. Freeman Junction is named after *my* father, your grandfather." "But he's dead Daddy." "Yes he is, but isn't it nice that he had this town named after him, and after us? We're the Freemans of Freeman Junction!"

As a teenager, in preparation to write a report on his supposed namesake town, Peter checked in the Bakersfield Public Library and found it not to be true. He didn't confront his father, allowing the false claim as simply a father's innocent encouragement of a child's fancy and humor, something he did especially with Peter's four sisters. But within the eulogy the Lawrence Freeman Produce Public Relations Department had written for Peter to read, there was a clear allegation that Lawrence's father had assisted Clare C. Miley in the 1920 formation of Freeman Junction. During Lawrence Freeman's funeral, Miley was still alive, 83 years old and living in Los Angeles, and he either didn't know or didn't care about the false credit Lawrence Freeman had given himself.

But Peter's love of the Old West never left him. His family had always visited Virginia City, Nevada, when they stayed in Lake Tahoe, and Peter had dragged a bored Kristi around

California, Nevada, and Arizona to look at whatever ghost towns he could find.

"Look at this!" Peter now exclaimed to Jay. "This is perfect! It looks...well, it looks fabricated, sure, like Frontierland at Disneyland, but it looks great! An Old West town by the sea. I've never seen it before, and I've driven up this way many times. How did I miss it?"

Jay clearly wasn't impressed, and barely looked around.

"Have you seen this before?" Peter asked him.

"Yeah I've been through here before," Jay nodded, not hiding his disinterest. "I didn't stay long. The man in the grocery store wouldn't return my greeting, and he practically threw my bag of granola and change on the counter. I got out of Dodge in a hurry."

"Maybe your long hair? You know how small towns are."

"No, it was something else."

Peter ignored Jay's remark as he studied the five buildings. "Look, even the 'Last Chance Gas Station and Garage.' How cool is that? Come on, let's check out the Saloon. It's after 12, I could use a beer."

Again Jay didn't respond, and Peter thought he recognized the reason for Jay's reluctance.

"Jay, are you an alcoholic?"

"Long reformed. I lost the taste for it, it

doesn't tempt me."

"I just want to go inside and have a look. I love Old West stuff."

"Are you sure Peter?" Jay looked at him earnestly. "I think we ought to just take off, get out of this town." But it was, after all, Peter's truck and Jay was just the hitchhiker.

"Well," Peter considered, "I'll just go inside for a bit. You can stay here. Maybe Barney needs water or a potty break." But Peter knew he'd done all that at the vista turnoff just 30 minutes earlier.

"No," Jay opened the passenger door. "I'd better go in with you."

The sight of the red, custom-striped four-wheel-drive Ford F-250 pickup making a sudden turn into the La Sangre Saloon caught Doyle Seeno's attention as he stood guard in front of the gas station. As he had just done with the small blue car he'd filled up, and with any car that stopped in town, he noted the truck's license plate and its frame that advertised the Serramonte Ford Dealer in San Francisco. The owner must have money, he deduced. The driver is a male, white, about 35, clean-cut but uppity, arrogant, of the world, walking with the devil. Even now, Doyle could see Satan in the passenger seat.

"So, Satan is your co-pilot huh?" Doyle

sneered, and he began to pray softly and righteously. "Lord protect us. If this sinner is sent from Satan or if he's demon-possessed, I pray you send him out of La Sangre and straight to hell!"

Doyle was satisfied. Yes, everything was in the hands of the Lord. If this...this uppity sinner, this demon...had come in to attack La Sangre, he would be dealt with. Maybe Doyle should run and warn the Pastor. No, Doyle remembered, the Pastor is in the Saloon having lunch with Sister Connie and Corey; he'll handle this demon from hell. The Pastor can kill him with one blow, like David killed Goliath.

The Saloon was empty except for the Satori family in the last booth on the right. Connie and Corey sat opposite Sal, their backs to the door. They heard the door open, and then watched as Sal's jaw dropped, his eyes widened, tightening the grip on his fork.

"Sal?" Connie asked.

Corey took his eyes off his father's horrified expression and turned around to see San Francisco Forty-Niners Running Back Pete Freeman seating himself at the counter. Corey turned back to his father.

"Hey Dad! That guy is..."

"Shutup!" Sal interrupted him with a hoarse whisper. "Shutup, you goddamn bastard!"

EIGHT

"I'll be right with you," Jessie glanced at Peter from the pass-through in the kitchen. Peter noticed that her glance lasted one second longer than it had to, and that she had ignored Jay. Okay, Peter just figured she recognized him, which wasn't unusual. He was sure that the threesome in the last booth, who were now making a hasty retreat out of the Saloon, had also noticed him, though the man had actually seemed shocked. Peter turned to Jay seated to his left to exchange a "Well, that's show-biz" smile, but Jay was watching the man as he was practically shoving the woman and boy towards the door. Peter followed Jay's glance and met eyes with the man. At the eye contact the man froze, weirdly furious. The woman and the kid, at the door, watched the deadlock in confusion.

"Sal?" the woman asked. The man didn't respond, but continued to drill his eyes into Peter.

All right, a sports freak, Peter figured, and turned back to the counter. Fans could be weird. And this guy might have been a fan of the Cincinnati Bengals, who had lost Superbowl XVI to the Forty-Niners. Peter's high yardage in that game made him an easy mark.

"Dad?" the kid ventured, causing Peter to turn again and look at the kid: tall, blonde, with confusion on his young handsome face. Peter gave the boy a friendly nod and smile, causing the man to physically force the boy and the woman out of the Saloon. The wooden door banged in finality.

"Did you see that?" Peter said to Jay. "I mean sure, I've been stared at before, but..."

Jay turned from the slammed door back to Peter. "Hey man, we really need to get out of here," he told him.

Peter noticed that Jay's normally placid face was furrowed. "Hey," he told Jay, "it was just a weird fan. I see them all the time. It's nothing."

"It's not just that. I said before Peter, this town isn't good. It's like that man who was hostile to me in the grocery store. This isn't a good place to be."

"I'm Jessie," the waitress stood in front of them, pulling out her pad. If she'd heard Jay's comments, she gave no sign. "What can I get you?"

"Oh," Peter turned to her, ignoring Jay's warning. "Well, I could use a beer, to start. For me anyway." Peter turned to Jay who, frown gone, was observing Jessie.

Jessie smirked and shook her head. "Sorry, the town's dry."

"What?"

"The town's dry. The only firewater around here is gas, which you can either buy at the over-priced pumps at the gas station, or listen to at the church."

"But the sign says 'Saloon.'"

"It's just a come-on. The Pastor," she nodded towards the door, "likes it. 'Lead them in with the temptation to sin,'" she raised her pad in mock preaching, "'and then lead them to the Lord.'" She smirked again at the door. "That was him that just left, with his old lady and kid. And now that he's gone..." She turned around to the counter and switched on the radio, and Johnny Lee began pleading forgiveness in the empty saloon. "I thought I was going to go nuts with them in here."

"That guy's a priest?"

"*Pastor*," she practically snarled. "*Pastor* Salvatore Satori." She paused, her smirk still intact. "To tell you the truth, I don't mind having to call him Pastor. If he listened carefully—which he never does—he'd realize that I'm not really saying Pastor, I'm actually saying 'bastard.' I'm able to say it exactly so that somebody has to decide for himself what word I'm using."

"Well, he sure looked at me funny," Peter understated, the Pastor's hostile glare still vivid.

"Like you were shit?"

Peter reacted with surprise, then just decided the profanity went with the territory of her being the waitress at a greasy diner in a small town. Except this girl wasn't fat and her light blonde hair didn't seem bleached. In fact she was very attractive; rather small with a natural body that matched her earthy personality. No, not earthy, her gross personality.

"I guess so," Peter responded. "Why did he leave like that?"

"Who knows, and who cares?" Jessie regarded the Saloon door in disgust.

"He left without paying."

"Honey, he *owns* this dump. He owns this whole damn town. He owns everything and everyone here except me, and tomorrow I'm going to be the first and only one to tell him that his shit smells like everyone else's."

Peter turned to Jay, who was watching her testimony, his face displaying no judgment.

"Anyway," Jessie said to Peter, "what do you want?"

"A beer." Actually I don't, Peter realized; it was just a knee-jerk response.

She smiled dryly. "Well, you're persistent anyway. The only thing I can offer you is Jack Daniels. At my place." She raised an eyebrow, clear and simple.

He was being hit on, again. Even if women

didn't know who Peter was, he knew that his looks encouraged hits, and it was getting old. In fact, it was more than old. As of today, that game wasn't just old, it was dead. As dead as his "relationship" with Kristi. As dead as Jay's alcoholism. Indeed, the second half of the game had begun.

"Peter," Jay said quietly, as if reading his thoughts. "Let's get out of here. Now."

It was disastrous, outside the Saloon. The fragile glass bubble that had held the Satori family together in a lovely-appearing, self-deluding vacuum had finally shattered, irreplaceable. Why, Connie wondered frantically, after all these years had it finally happened? She had worked so hard to maintain the status quo, and now, for some inexplicable reason, her best efforts at keeping the family on a delicately even keel were nothing but vain and hopeless, quickly destroyed a minute ago by...Peter Freeman, of the San Francisco Forty-Niners.

"Go home!" Sal ordered her brusquely. "You too!" he snapped at Corey.

"No!" Corey retorted. His long-held reserve had burst. It was over.

Both his parents raised their eyes at Corey's boldness, his mother surprised, his father shocked. It had never happened before.

Corey didn't care. He just got a scholarship

for Bethany Bible College, four years no less, and like it or not, his father no longer had any power over him, and he knew that Sal knew it. ("Shutup, you goddamn bastard!") The words were still audible, to all three of them. The final break.

"I'm going back in there," Corey stated simply. "I want to meet him." Sal's glare had lost any power it may have had over Corey. And in fact, it never did have any power over him.

Sal gave one last desperate cry: "GET HOME, YOU...."

"SAL!" Connie cut him off. Sal had never hit Corey, at her insistence, but while he could be verbally abusive, this was the first time he'd used profanity.

"And you get home too!" Sal turned on her. "Don't ask questions, just go!" He looked over at the La Sangre Garage, his eyes narrowing in determination. "I have to see Doyle about something, and then I'm coming home." He turned back to Corey, knowing he'd lost him. There was no more he could do. But he still had Connie, and he turned to her in a final absurd effort of control, a return to his Order. "We have to get ready for the Father's Day picnic tomorrow!"

Connie looked at Corey. Father's Day Picnic indeed, their eyes spoke. Given what had just happened it would be hilarious if it wasn't so pathetic. Without a word Corey turned and walked back into the Saloon.

Connie made herself not call after him. He was gone, and the slam of the Saloon door confirmed it. The only solace she had was that their connection was still intact. At least she still had that.

Jay and Peter both turned at the sound of the slamming door and saw Corey, who hesitated just inside the doorway.

"Peter, let's get out of here," Jay repeated as if it was their last chance. "We'll head further north."

"Excuse me," Corey said, approaching Peter, who acknowledged him with a friendly, if confused, smile. "You're Pete Freeman, aren't you? Of the San Francisco Forty-Niners?"

"Yes I am," Peter extended his hand.

"I'm sorry to bother you," Corey shook his hand enthusiastically. "I know you must get bothered all the time."

"Not at all," Peter said sincerely. "Sit down," he motioned to the stool on the other side of him.

"Thanks." Corey sat down gratefully.

"What's your name?"

"Me? I'm Corey. Corey Satori. My middle name is Peter, like yours."

"Oh yeah?"

"My Dad chose my first name, and my Mom

chose my middle name."

"So Corey," Peter asked the obviously star-struck kid, "you were just in here, weren't you? I saw you in the booth back there." In an effort to try to get conversation going, Peter didn't consider that his mention of that scene, whatever it was, would embarrass the kid. Oh well, too late.

"Oh...yeah...with my Mom and Dad. We had to kind of leave in a hurry. But I just wanted to come back and tell you what a great running back you were...I mean, you *are*."

Peter smiled at Corey's correction. "Thanks Corey, but you were right the first time. I'm retired.

"Well," Corey looked at Peter's right hand, at the Superbowl ring. "Well you did it anyway, and I thought you were great."

"What *is* this?" Jessie asked Peter impatiently. "Are you someone famous?"

Peter had forgotten about her, but Jay hadn't. He had been studying her, and must have given up on his insistence they leave. Now he seemed to have other things on his mind.

"Oh come on Jessie!" Corey admonished her. "This is Pete Freeman, running back for the San Francisco Forty-Niners!"

"*Retired* running back," Peter corrected.

"Oh," Jessie shrugged it off. "I don't follow baseball anymore." She saw Peter and Corey exchange amused smiles.

"Football, Jessie," Corey said.

The boy's mild correction turned Jessie's boredom into anger. "Retired?" she showed the same disgust she had when describing the Pastor. "So, if you were making all that money, why'd you quit? Too old, huh?"

Peter wasn't taken aback, but the girl's response reminded him of his conversation with Kristi just a few hours earlier. ("I just want you to be happy," he'd told Kristi. "Sure Pete," she'd responded, "whatever *that* is.") Both girls were waitresses at different restaurants, about the same age, the same general look. But unlike Kristi, who still had hope, for this girl, it was over.

Jessie responded to Peter's observation by slamming her pad and pencil down in front of him. "Here, football player," she snapped. "Give the kid your autograph and either order something or get the hell out of here!"

Corey stared at Jessie. He'd never seen her this way; she had a smirk on her face as if "Oh, I'm just kidding." But she wasn't. She was actually attacking Pete, like she needed to...destroy him for some reason. In fact, she was acting towards Pete just like Sal had just acted towards Pete, and himself. ("Shutup, you goddamn bastard!") What is going on? It's some kind of crazy day in La Sangre.

"Peter." Jay had stood up behind him, his hand on his shoulder. "Let's go." At the touch

Peter turned around. He had almost forgotten about Jay.

"Yeah," Peter nodded. "Yeah, you're right." This kid was great, and inexplicably Peter didn't want to leave him like this, but this was a crazy place, a crazy town, like Jay had warned him. We have to get out. "Well, it was great to meet you Corey," Peter shook hands with him.

"Same here, Mr. Freeman."

"Pete."

"Pete," Corey beamed.

Peter got up from the stool and walked out of the Saloon, with Jay and Corey following.

Jessie watched their exit. She wanted to feel triumphant, like she had with the Pastor earlier today, but her face was furrowed. Why did she have to attack the football player, and Corey? She'd never attacked Corey before, especially being the Pastor's son. What if he told his father about her behavior? It wasn't a smart move. And she was always smart. But now, this weekend, she was losing control, just when she needed it most, for what she had to do.

It wasn't until Connie reached the house that her tears began, a steady stream from behind the solid dam of protection she had long built and maintained. The dam didn't burst wide open, not after 17 years of a staunch image of the serene Pastor's wife. Yet the dam was indeed collapsing, brick by brick. Just minutes earlier, in the Saloon, Sal had ripped the first brick out from the very bottom of the dam, and now the others were straining, cracking, and giving way.

It had been coming all along, Connie O'Hara Satori, she told herself as she walked inside the house and up the stairs to Corey's room. And the closer it had come, the more frantically you kept adding bricks to the dam, shoring up any truth about this home, your husband, your family, the whole town of La Sangre.

In Corey's room she pulled a suitcase out of the closet, and with tears still running at their even flow, she began packing for him. Socks, underwear, two pairs of jeans....

What was she doing? Why was she packing Corey's suitcase?

Because he's leaving, Connie, and not just to that room above the La Sangre Garage. He got a four year scholarship, remember? But after what happened today, in the Saloon, and outside, Corey would have left La Sangre anyway. A destination wasn't necessary, her son was gone.

She fell against the side of the bed and slid onto the floor, the dam collapsing and the steady stream of tears turning into a long-neglected gush of pain and loneliness that was the long-forgotten Connie O'Hara.

"Oh God!" she cried out. "Help me! Please God, please! Help me!"

Unseen, Lillian had watched the exchange between the Satori family from inside the General Store. Father's Day weekend was officially here, she realized in fear. It had started as fear this morning, then turned into anticipation, then excitement. Now it was back to fear. And anger. As she watched a destroyed Connie cross the highway towards the bluff, she was tempted to say to herself, "You've had it coming, *Mrs. Salvatore Satori!*"

But she stopped herself and grabbed what could be her first and last chance to finally do something in this town. Maybe there had been a purpose for her being in La Sangre after all, and it had finally arrived.

She watched as the Pastor went over to the Garage and used his power over Doyle to give him some kind of orders, and after Sal left towards the bluff, Lillian knew it was time to move. She couldn't spend another minute in the La Sangre General Store, wondering if her life was over. Or if it was, she would go down fighting.

Lillian closed and locked the door, ignoring the "Be back by..." plastic sign with its clock face and movable hands, and strode determinedly down the wooden walkway to the dirt road that led down to the bluff. Ahead of her Sal had walked directly to the cliff, not north to his house. That was good, because finally, at last, she was going to talk to Connie Satori, and Connie was going to listen, and talk, to her.

Sal walked south along the cliff out of sight of his home. He couldn't face his wife, couldn't go back to his home after what had happened.

But he had been unable to stop himself. Satan had come into him and made him powerless over his own senses, his body, his mouth. He'd spoken the unspeakable, and there was no way to take it back. ("Shutup, you goddamn bastard!")

"Lord help me!" Sal screamed at the ocean, which beat against the rocks. "I couldn't stop myself! Why didn't you stop me?"

How could I, Sal, when you were so hell-bent on unleashing your fury?

"Then why didn't you make me stop myself?" Sal screamed.

Because you didn't want to stop Sal. You've wanted to do that for a long time.

"Lord God in heaven!" Sal screamed. "Father, help me! Help me Father God!"

But the ocean just beat against the rocks below.

You figure it out Sal.

Peter turned to Jay once they were outside in front of the Saloon. "That was really weird in there," he said, "that crazy waitress. What was that all about?"

Jay only shook his head but Corey responded. "Yeah, I don't know. I've never seen Jessie act like that. If my Dad ever knew she talked that way to the customers..."

Peter looked at Corey and then Jay, who had walked over to the passenger door of the pickup. "Come on Peter," Jay said. In the back of the pickup, Barney looked at Peter with the same sense of urgency.

Peter stepped off the walkway and to his pickup, his mind loaded with the Pastor and his iron stare, Jessie and her negativity. And now Corey, who seemed like a good kid, but who needed something from him that he wasn't in a position to give. Jay was right, this place was not good.

"Yeah," Peter finally said. "Let's get out of Dodge." From the bed of the pickup, Barney gave an agreeable bark. "That's right Barney, we're getting out of La Sangre." He gave Barney a pat on the head and got in the cab, put the key into the ignition and turned it.

And the truck wouldn't start. Nothing. Totally dead. Peter tried it three times but no luck.

"What the hell?" Peter pulled the hood latch and got out, followed by Jay.

"What's wrong?" Corey asked as Peter opened the hood.

"Look!" Jay pointed.

"Someone stole my battery," Peter said.

Barney growled in warning.

"Connie?" Lillian's voice called from downstairs.

Connie was still sitting on the floor in Corey's bedroom.

"Are you up there?" Lillian called again.

Yes, I am, Connie said to herself. Connie is here. The real Connie is finally here.

"I'm coming up," Lillian announced.

Connie heard Lillian's footsteps on the stairs, firm and determined. They reached the landing, hesitated, and then as if directed, came down the hallway to Corey's room.

"Connie?" Lillian stood in the doorway, looking at a frightened, childlike Connie seated on the floor, leaning against the bed, arms wrapped around herself, a tear-stained face staring up at her. On the bed was an open, half-packed suitcase. "Connie?" she said again, her nurse's training kicking in. Give her space. Let her tell you what happened.

"Lillian," Connie looked at her, wondering at the new tone of her own voice, at the disappearance of its well-modulated reserve. "I've been waiting so long for you to come here like this. I was afraid that you weren't going to come up the stairs, that you were going to go away."

"I'm here now," Lillian said gently.

"It all fell apart today," Connie shook her head. "But the funny thing is, I'm glad. I can't live like that anymore."

"I'm glad too," Lillian nodded, maintaining her nurse's tone. "I know what you mean."

"But now I'm afraid too, Lillian. I'm afraid that he'll tear this town apart." And Connie wondered whom she meant, Sal or the football player. She had meant Sal, but she was thinking about Peter Freeman. "But I also hope it happens. It *has* to happen."

"What has to happen?" Lillian was suddenly chilled but she kept her nurse's tone. "And who is going to tear the town apart?"

"Sal...or Peter Freeman."

"Peter Freeman?"

"The football player."

Lillian shook her head. She didn't follow sports. "What football player?"

"He came into town about twenty minutes ago."

Lillian always maintained a vigil of vehicles that stopped in La Sangre, just to pass the time if nothing else. "Was he driving a red pickup truck?"

"Yes."

"How...will he tear the town apart?"

"He made Sal call Corey a goddamn bastard!"

Lillian shook her head again, her nurse's

reserve turning into confusion, and that still-unnamed fear taking form. How could anyone force the Pastor into using profanity? she wondered, although somehow it didn't surprise her. She knew that nothing would surprise her this weekend. Connie was right when she said "It has to happen."

"So," Lillian tried to sound casual, "Sal cursed at Corey." But the image of the half-smashed bakery cake that read "Congratulations Corey" hit her. ("We all have to go sometime," Jessie had declared.)

"You see," Connie took a deep breath. She had to say it. It was time. "Sal knows, but Corey doesn't, that Sal isn't his real father. Corey is illegitimate."

NINE

Peter looked over at the La Sangre Gas Station, where Doyle Seeno leaned against the gas pump in his dirty white uniform, watching them intently. Peter turned to Corey. "Do you think he'd have a battery?"

"He should. I've seen him replace people's batteries before. Let's ask."

"Yeah, and maybe he saw something. Somebody hanging around my truck." Stolen batteries were not uncommon in San Francisco, and Peter had left his driver door unlocked when he parked in front of the Saloon. It would have taken just a minute to pull the hood latch and remove the battery. The Saloon had no front windows.

Peter followed Corey up the walkway to the gas station. Doyle watched them motionless, as if expecting them.

"You have a problem?" Doyle asked Peter superciliously, relishing his position of power.

"Somebody just stole my battery. Did you see anyone at my truck? We've been in the Saloon."

Doyle took too long to respond. His power at the La Sangre Last Chance Gas Station and Garage always felt good. He savored it.

"Just answer him Doyle!" Corey spoke up, as surprised with his new bravado as Doyle was. But after today, what had happened with his father (with "Sal," Corey silently referred to him for the first time), and with the presence of Pete Freeman, Corey was flexing his newfound freedom. And it felt good. His new life had begun.

"No," Doyle answered the question simply. Volunteer nothing, he told himself, but be nice, be Christian. Corey was, after all, the Pastor's son.

"No what?" Peter remained polite. He knew he had to be careful with small-towners, especially if they knew who he was. "No, you didn't see anyone at my truck, or no, you don't have a battery?"

"No to both," was Doyle's smug reply.

"Have you been here, outside, all this time?" Peter asked.

"In and out."

"Pete," Corey said, "it's happened here before, once or twice. A driver's battery is old, they see someone parked, and if there's no one around or no traffic, they swipe their battery."

"Yeah," Peter nodded, "it happens all the time in the city, on older cars with no hood latches."

"The city," Doyle repeated sarcastically, like it was the most evil thing in the world.

Peter ignored the sarcasm. "Look, I've got Triple-A, they can bring one out." He turned to Corey. "Is there a phone I can use? Where are we, 'La Sanger?'"

Peter's mispronunciation caused Doyle to explode, with or without the Pastor's son present. "La *Sahn*-gree!" Doyle fairly spit the words out. "La *Sahn*-gree!" he glared at Peter with hate. "Don't you know what that *means*?"

"Shutup Doyle!" Corey raised his voice. "Just call the AAA station in Santa Rosa!"

Peter looked at Corey. Jay had been right. Let's just get out of here. "Thanks Corey," he told him. He pulled out his wallet and handed his AAA card to Doyle, but Doyle just looked at it.

"Doyle!" Corey demanded.

He shrugged ceremoniously. "The phones are out."

"What?" Corey said.

"We can't dial out. Mary just told me."

Corey turned to Peter. "There's only one phone line in or out of town. Mary is the operator. She receives and transfers all calls out of her home."

"Isn't there regular phone service here?" Peter asked. What kind of town is this? he wondered.

"It's how my Dad wants it," Corey said as if reading Peter's mind. "You have to go through Mary to make or receive any calls."

"It's how the Pastor wants it," Doyle proclaimed, glaring at Peter.

"When will the problem be fixed?" Peter asked Corey.

"It'll be fixed when it's fixed," Doyle replied, still glaring at Peter.

Connie and Lillian sat in the Satori kitchen, comforted with tea and in the definite turf of La Sangre women.

"I was pregnant with Corey before I met Sal," Connie explained. "But he knew, I told him."

"Why did you marry him?" Lillian asked the question as simply as she could, with no judgment.

Connie took no offense to the question, but was thoughtful, remembering. "I'd like to say it was love," she reflected, "but it was mostly gratitude. I was 17, raised in a Norman Rockwell home in Bakersfield with loving Christian parents, prayers before meals and at bedtime, and church on Sunday. I had an older brother and younger sister. I guess there was some of the middle-child syndrome—I wasn't an aggressive boy like my brother and I wasn't cute like my sister."

"You're pretty," Lillian said, noticing she felt

no envy. In a flashback to this morning, she remembered that she always used to envy, even be jealous of, pretty women, but today, strangely, she wasn't. Maybe that was over for her. She hoped so.

"Now I am, pretty," Connie smiled. "Anyway, a high school boy I went out with, just once..." She shook her head and looked at Lillian. "How do those things happen, when we don't even consider them? Are they allowed to happen? Are they *supposed* to happen? I know I had a choice in the matter, and yet it just happened." Connie stopped and sipped her tea. She was enjoying the talk, the connection; it was long overdue. "So, I got pregnant, after that one time. My parents were shocked, of course, but they supported me, and sent me to stay with an aunt in Fresno—that's what you did in those days—and there I met Sal. At that time there was more softness to him, a simplicity, an easy directness. And perhaps most importantly, he took charge. I liked that, the way he took charge."

Lillian gave a half-smile. "Well, *that* hasn't changed."

"No," Connie agreed, "but it's gotten worse. Back then he knew what he wanted and he went for it. He told me that he liked me...and he did, I know he did. I felt so ashamed, that he should like me; at first of course he didn't know I was pregnant, and here he was the Associate Pastor of a church and was expecting to become a Pastor, somewhere. I told him that I was pregnant, and couldn't marry the father. But," she smiled at the memory, "he just looked at me as if it didn't matter, and he asked me to marry him. And I liked how he...again, took charge. I didn't have to worry about anything. Sal was wiser and a few years older than I, he would take care of me."

"Well, that's always nice," Lillian looked down at her teacup, wondering if she'd ever had a man take charge in her life besides her father. Well, there was one man, in Seattle, years ago, but he sure didn't take charge, even though she thought he did. "Did Sal ask you who the father was?"

"No. I didn't volunteer it and we never discussed it. I don't think he wanted to know. That made it easier, and besides, Corey's father was out of my life."

"So you married Sal," Lillian said.

Connie looked up at Lillian for a moment, grateful at the new friendship. Lillian was looking down at her teacup, and Connie looked back down at hers. Amazing what a cup of tea can do. "I think...I think the reason I married Sal was that my getting pregnant, my mistake..." Connie stopped herself. *Was* it a mistake? She had never thought so. "Well, being pregnant was a part of me that Sal accepted. It wasn't something separate from me, some disassociated 'thing' that had to be forgiven. It was me, and Sal accepted me that way. I appreciated that, and I was grateful to him."

"That's pretty impressive Connie, for any man to do that. And a Pastor no less." Lillian considered her next question, and then proceeded. "But...did you love him?"

Connie looked at her, wondering. "Lillian, I just realized that I don't know what love is. Do you?"

Lillian took a deep breath. "No," she exhaled, thinking of Seattle. "I used to think I did, but no, I don't."

"Well," Connie went on, "we got married right away, not to pretend that the baby was his—it would have been an eight-pound seven-month baby anyway, no point in denying it. And Sal would have dared anyone to confront him with it."

"Well, that's something else that hasn't changed, his fearlessness."

Connie nodded. "It's a good quality in him, in anyone. But somehow it turned into a need to control. It all started when Corey was born. Sal's face suddenly turned hard, his shoulders and his walk seemed to stiffen. The softness was gone. It was fine when my pregnancy by someone else was abstract, but when Corey was born, the reality of him not being Sal's own son finally hit him. I know he wanted his own child, his own son."

"You never got pregnant again?" Lillian asked.

Connie looked up at Lillian. "No. I got checked out, and I'm fine. I can have all the babies I want."

"And Sal?"

"He won't get examined."

Corey followed Peter back to his truck.

"Where's Jay?" Peter looked around. "Oh, maybe he went back into the Saloon to use the bathroom."

"Who's Jay?" Corey asked.

"The guy that was with me."

"What guy?"

Peter looked at the kid. "You saw him. The big guy, red hair, red beard, red plaid jacket."

Corey shook his head.

Peter looked in the bed of his truck. "His backpack is gone! The dog is gone!"

"Whose backpack? What dog? I don't understand, who are you talking about?"

Peter looked at Corey again. "The guy that was with me! You were sitting in the booth in the Saloon, you turned and saw me walk in with him. We sat at the counter. You sat on the other side of me from him." Am I going crazy? Peter wondered.

Corey just shook his head again, and Peter thought maybe the kid was so starstruck he'd ignored Jay altogether.

"Pete..." Corey began helplessly.

Peter waited, suddenly thrust back into the abyss he'd felt at the Golden Gate Bridge. "What?" he asked the boy, somehow fearing the answer.

"You walked into the Saloon alone."

TEN

Sal stood in the kitchen doorway. The sight of his wife and Lillian Walker at the table, leaning towards each other in earnest conversation, was another below-the-belt blow to the day's calamities. He didn't have to say anything to the women. His expression of "What the hell is going on here?" was unmistakable.

Lillian looked at Sal. While he still irritated her, she remembered something her mother had told her: when you know somebody's history you can't hate them. But she only had the second half of Sal's history, from the time he'd met Connie. Who was the man—the boy—who lived before that time?

"Lillian and I are having tea," Connie answered Sal's unspoken question. The boldness of her reply surprised them both.

"I can see that. Tea and sympathy, it looks like." Sal's unnecessarily nasty remark took him from ridiculous to pathetic, and even he knew it. Why am I acting this way? he thought helplessly.

Lillian decided it was her time to speak. This

wasn't her home, wasn't her marriage, but it was her time, finally, here in La Sangre, to speak up. "What we're doing is Biblical," she told Sal.

Sal ignored Lillian's remark. "And who's doing the preparation for the Father's Day picnic?"

The Father's Day picnic. From ridiculous to pathetic to laughable. Lillian hoped Connie saw it too.

Connie delayed her response with a deep breath, a far cry from the quick dutiful answers she usually gave Sal. "When Lillian and I are through, I'm going to meet with the ladies."

Sal turned to Lillian. "In the meantime, who's minding the General Store?"

Enough, Lillian said to herself. You made a vow this morning that you were going to fight, even if it meant going down fighting. Not hating somebody is one thing, but putting up with their abuse is another. The battle is on, it's your last stand, Lillian Walker. Fight the battle, and then leave this town, as you should have done years ago.

"I closed up the store so I could talk to Connie about something," Lillian said, more slowly than she had to.

"Talk to her about what?"

"Frankly Pastor, it's none of your business," Lillian carefully increased her tempo and sharpened her tone. "But if you must insist, I was seeking counsel, as the Bible tells us to. 'We are to seek counsel within the Body.' Connie and I talked, and we were just going to pray together when you walked in. It was to be a private prayer, between the two of us, and God. We were going to pray for anointing, and wisdom, and peace. You see, Pastor Satori, I found myself under an attack by Satan, right there on the walkway in front of the General Store, for desires of the flesh, and I needed to be prayed for, and for hands to be laid upon me, that this attack might cease and that I might walk in the Spirit, not in the flesh."

Sal stared at her, speechless, as Lillian stood up and prepared to leave. Nurse Walker was tempted by the flesh? his expression read.

"Does it surprise you, Pastor, that I should be under attack by Satan for desires of the flesh? I may be unattractive and nearing 50 years old, but somehow I find that I am still capable of sin." She paused for emphasis. "As we all are, aren't we Pastor?"

Sal continued to stare at her. Who was this woman?

Lillian waited for a response from him, and when there was none, she continued, intoxicated by the showdown, and buoyed by Connie's shocked expression.

"As it turned out, Connie and I didn't have time to pray, Pastor," she went on. "If so, I would have asked her to lay hands on me, and to anoint me with oil. It would have to be plain old Crisco oil, from the cupboard, but the Bible doesn't specify which brand to use, does it?"

Lillian walked out of the kitchen and out of the Satori house.

Peter sat heavily on the steps of the Saloon, blood rushing out of his head. He took a few deep breaths, and with the self-aid training of an NFL player, he put his head between his knees.

Corey watched helplessly, then sat down next to Peter. After a few seconds he tentatively put a hand on Peter's shoulder. "Hey Pete, are you all right?"

Peter took another deep breath, and after a moment he raised his head. He wasn't going to pass out, but he'd better be careful, move slowly. "I don't know, I think so. I just have to look back, on this morning, on what happened..."

"I can go ask my Mom, or Sal. Maybe they noticed him with you, maybe I didn't. All that time I was just looking at you, surprised to see you here. Or I can go inside the Saloon and ask Jessie. Yeah, I never thought about her."

Peter turned back to the Saloon, not wanting to go back inside. Jessie was somehow dangerous to him, or just plain dangerous, period. ("Let's just get out of this town," Jay had said, "before it's too late.")

"You go ask her," Peter told Corey.

Corey got up and went inside the Saloon while Peter sat, with the emptiness, the darkness from the morning engulfing him. His life was again in a delicate balance, like when he was at the Golden Gate Bridge, stuck in halftime. Then Jay had appeared and everything made sense. But that was some kind of fantasy now, wasn't it? Had Peter been driving north on Highway 1, along the Pacific Ocean, all alone? Just like Jay had "walked all the way down Sunset Boulevard to the Pacific Ocean."

Corey came back within a minute and sat down next to Peter. "I asked her if that man who was with you had come back in, and she said 'What man?' And then she started to laugh."

Peter turned to him. "She laughed? Like it was a joke? Maybe she *did* see him and she lied about it."

"No," Corey shook his head. Yes, Jessie was acting like a crazy lady, but he was sure she wasn't lying. (Unless she's a good liar, Corey.) "No," Corey said again.

I'm going to figure this out, Peter told himself. I swear to God I'm going to figure this out. It can't be over, not yet. It must make sense, it has to. He sat still, looking around, gathering his resources. It was no different from the times he'd been sacked on the field, the wind knocked out of him, and then suddenly found himself sitting on the bench, disoriented and confused, forgetting what the score was, even what team they were playing and what city they were in. A mesh of jerseys and helmets milling around the sidelines, the crowd sounding like a distant roar. He could hear it even now, the crowd roaring....

No, it was the ocean, just a hundred yards away (the length of a football field), beating against the cliff, steady and insistent.

"I'm going to figure this out," Peter made himself speak aloud. He stood up carefully, and with a definite plan, he walked slowly and deliberately to his truck. He looked inside the cab, sure there would be some clue, some proof of Jay's existence.

There was nothing on the seat, the passenger seat belt was neatly in its rolled-up position, there was no discernible impression on the upholstery. Now don't lose it completely Pete, it's leather, it never shows an imprint.

He looked in the bed. No sign that a backpack or a dog had been there. What about dog hair? None. Okay, so Barney didn't shed, he tried to tell himself.

Come on Peter, an Irish Setter that doesn't shed? And just how did you come up with the name Barney for the dog? That's a pretty complete fantasy, isn't it? ("It's short for Barnabas," Jay had told him.)

Corey walked over to Peter, watching him, feeling pain for him, yet a sense of manhood in a new responsibility. Pete Freeman, Running Back for the San Francisco Forty-Niners, was his friend. Corey was helping him. Indeed,his life had started today, when Pete had walked into the Saloon, and when his father—when Sal—had given him license to leave. ("You god-damn bastard!")

"Maybe," Corey ventured, "maybe you pulled over and took a nap, while you were driving up here, and the whole thing was a dream, one of those dreams that seem real, and you're not sure, even after you wake up, if it was real or not. I've had dreams like that."

"Maybe," Peter nodded, searching for some-thing, anything concrete to hang onto. There had to be a clue, unless...

He looked around La Sangre, at the General Store across the street, at the Grocery Store next to it. He visualized Corey's father forcing a retreat out of the Saloon when he walked in, the crazy waitress, crazy and, yes, evil. Maybe... ("I've never seen this town before, and I've driv-en up this way many times," he'd told Jay. "How could I have missed it?") Maybe...

Maybe I'm still dreaming. It seems just as real as my time with Jay. But maybe my time with Jay wasn't real, and so this isn't real either, and I'm stuck in it. ("Like being stuck in half-time," he'd told Jay.) How had Jay responded to that? Maybe there was a clue in something Jay had said.

("Cracked up," Jay had plainly stated. "Had a nervous breakdown. Right there on Sunset Boulevard.")

"You want to walk around a bit?" Corey asked Peter. "You might feel a little better. Or maybe you ought to lie down. I've got a room of my own now, up over the Garage. You can lie down there for a while."

("Cracked up. Had a nervous breakdown.")

"Pete, do you want to lie down?" Corey asked again.

Peter looked at Corey and shook his head. If he were to lie down, he might give in to it. Like lying down on the field after he'd been sacked. He had to get up, had to walk, so that he would run again. Walk before you run. "Maybe a walk," he managed to say to Corey.

"Sure," Corey said, placing a hand on Peter's back. "We can walk over to the cliff, by the ocean."

("I walked all the way down Sunset Boulevard," Jay had told him, "all the way to the ocean.")

Walk to the ocean? On *Sunset* Boulevard? Kristi had been into dreams, the only thing she discussed that was in any way spiritual. Was Jay's story, his walking to the ocean on Sunset Boulevard a symbol, a way of saying Highway 1? The "sun set" along Highway 1.

Peter looked up and down Highway 1,

noticing that there was no traffic. Had he seen any traffic at all since he had left Highway 101 and gone through Muir Woods? Did he get "lost in the woods?"

Peter had been accused by various coaches and teammates, and many times by Kristi, and his father especially, that he "thinks too much." Only during a game, with the clock running and especially when he had the ball in his hands did he stop thinking and just run, magically finding those openings ("Like Moses parting the Red Sea," Jay had reminded him.) So, was he *thinking* too much now?

Golden Gate Bridge. Maybe he'd passed through some "golden gate?" And he had "crossed the Bridge," met Jay, and then he'd left Highway 101. They were going to go north together, on Route 1. Route *One*.

Thinking too much again Peter?

But somehow it all made sense.

"Do you want to walk to the ocean?" Corey asked him again.

("The only reason I stopped at the ocean," Jay had said, "was because I couldn't walk on the water.")

Was Jay actually Peter himself? Had he been warning himself that this was going to happen? If so, he can't walk to the ocean, to the cliff, because then he would...

("Crack up. Have a nervous breakdown.")

"Let's go walk to the ocean," Corey said gently, adding pressure with his hand to Peter's back.

Maybe it's worse than a nervous breakdown. Maybe I died.

"Pete?" Corey asked.

He had died in a car crash, that was it. And now he was in hell. That Pastor was the devil. The girl in the Saloon had practically told him that. ("Bastard!" she'd referred to him.)

"Pete?" Corey's voice echoed a mile away.

No, the kid is here, he's real. I didn't die, I just...

"...cracked up..."

"Pete, sit back down," the kid's voice now several miles away.

"...had a nervous breakdown..."

And Peter began to slip.

On her way down the walkway back to the General Store, Lillian Walker recognized the signs of a fainting spell from the good-looking young man—that must be the football player, what was his name, Peter?—leaning against the red pickup truck, accompanied by Corey. Her nurse's instinct kicked in, she quickened her pace, then ran, as she saw him wavering, no blood in his face, his eyes rolling upwards.

She got to him and she and Corey caught him before he hit the ground.

ELEVEN

"What was *that* all about?" Sal demanded of his wife after Lillian left.

Connie looked at Sal, feeling very tired. How am I going to live with him after Corey leaves? Was Corey the only reason I've stayed here? That's the issue, plain and simple. Now Corey has a full college scholarship, he'll be leaving. All the effort she'd spent to keep the family in a proper appearance before the town had been her duty as the "Pastor's Wife." But now it was over, leaving her feeling very tired.

"Well?" Sal's voice boomed through the kitchen.

Connie fought to keep her voice level. "Sal, I want to go down to Bakersfield, to see my parents." She would go to Bakersfield, and then stay there. She would never come back to La Sangre.

"All right. We can go down there next week for a couple of days. But right now I'm asking you about that scene with Lillian. She's acting strangely."

Lillian, acting strangely? Connie wished

Lillian was still around to hear that. She'd have something to say about it.

Come on Connie, fight your own battles.

"No," Connie shook her head. "You'll have to talk to Lillian yourself about that 'scene.' But I want to go down to Bakersfield to visit my parents, alone."

"Alone!" What the *hell* is going on in his town? Sal wondered, frustrated. People were supposed to answer *his* questions, especially his wife. "Why?" he asked Connie. It was a general question, not just why is she going alone to Bakersfield, but why was all this happening?

"I just want to, Sal." And you won't ever have to see me again, she said to herself. You'll have to explain that to the town yourself.

"Just what were you and Lillian talking about? Were you talking about our family? Personal things about us? About Corey? You weren't going to pray, were you? You weren't going to lay hands on her, you weren't going to anoint her with oil!"

"Lillian told you! I was seeking counsel!"

"Lillian said *she* was seeking counsel from *you*! You'd better get your stories straight. You're the Pastor's wife! You don't..." Sal stopped himself.

"I don't *what* Sal? *I* can't seek counsel? Because I'm the Pastor's wife, I'm above that? Sal," she looked at him in a plea, "maybe it's just possible that I'm not happy!"

"NOT HAPPY?"

Connie stared at him. The inference was clear: how could she even *think* such a thing, let alone say it.

Because Connie, here in La Sangre you just repeat to yourself over and over, like a Christian robot, "I am happy. I am happy." You don't question it, never mind that you don't even know what happiness is.

Sal waited, his shouted inquiry ringing throughout the kitchen, throughout the house. He suddenly wondered if any neighbors might have heard it. Nobody outside of Connie and Corey had ever heard him shout. He would raise his voice to others when necessary, but definitely not shout. Even this morning in the Saloon, he'd kept his volume low. ("Shutup, you goddamn bastard!")

Connie looked away from Sal and down at her teacup, wondering incongruously if this is where the practice of reading tea leaves had originated. A reading of the truth.

All right Connie, you have to look at yourself, and don't play victim. Think of what you've done to Sal, not what he may have done to you. First of all, did you place Corey, your son, ahead of Sal?

Yes, she nodded.

From the start?

Yes, right from the start.

So in Sal's great need for love, you've failed him. That may be the reason he created what you silently refer to as the La Sangre Christian Theme Park. Sal needed love and acceptance, and when he didn't get it from you, he thought he could get it by manufacturing a place where happiness is contrived, and where personal responsibility and choice are unnecessary. All anyone has to do is pay the admission fee of their own identity, hop on a ride, and anything good like flying through the air on Dumbo is of God, and anything bad like the wicked witch in the Snow White ride is of Satan. And the Bible is a children's storybook that force-feeds the reader contrived and predictable feelings and reactions, like a laugh track on a TV sitcom or the applause on a game show. Connie, you enabled Sal in making La Sangre what it is today, a paper mache world of fantasy.

"Oh God!" Connie cried. "Sal, I'm sorry! It's my fault! I failed you!"

Sal softened and sat down at the kitchen table across from his wife, shoving Lillian's near-empty teacup aside. "Let's pray about it," he said gently.

"No Sal! I don't want to pray, I'm tired of praying with you. I want to *talk*!"

"We'll pray," he said instead, taking Connie's hands in his.

Peter woke up on a cot in the First Aid room at the rear of the General Store. On the opposite wall was a photo-poster of a rugged seascape, the Northern California or Oregon coast. He wondered how it was that he rarely visited the Northern California coast, drove up through the Redwoods, as he had...today? Was it just today that he'd driven through Muir Woods? He and Jay?

Peter raised his head. Jay.

After being asleep, it seemed more like a dream now than it had earlier today. That must be it, it was a very clear, very realistic dream. They're that way sometimes. So he hadn't had an accident, hadn't died, and La Sangre, strange as it appeared to be, wasn't hell. Not yet anyway. ("We have to get out of here, Peter," he'd been warned.)

He lay his head back on the pillow. Soft and comfortable. It was peaceful here. Nice. He read the inscription at the bottom of the seascape poster: "Today is the first day of the rest of your life."

He'd seen that and heard it many times, it was as popular during the 1970s as "Have A Nice Day." But this time he really considered the words. "The rest of my life," he said out loud. Maybe he wasn't stuck in halftime any more, and this was the beginning of the second half.

But what's the score?

"It doesn't matter," he could imagine Jay saying, "as long as you're in the game."

Jay again.

No, I'll just rest now. We'll talk about it later, me and that lady—the nurse—and that kid. What's his name? Corey. They're both real, and they seem okay, not crazy like the waitress and gas station guy and that Pastor. The nurse—yes, Lillian is her name, she had talked to him before he went to sleep—had she given him something, to sleep, to relax him? He couldn't remember. But he was all right, physically, Lillian had told him, as she took his temperature, checked his pulse and blood pressure. He was just exhausted. He had a lot of things on his mind, she'd said, especially since his father had just died. The hitchhiker, real or not, was his mind's way of coping. We can talk about it later, she assured him.

Had Peter told her about Jay? Yes, they did have a long talk. And Lillian explained that people often go through this after a death. He'd had a collapse, but it's nothing to worry about. He just needed to rest. To relax. La Sangre, with the ocean and fresh air, was a good place to rest and relax, she had told him. But Peter had noticed a hint of doubt, even sarcasm, in her voice, and she noticed that he noticed. "Just rest and relax," she repeated without the doubt or sarcasm, covering for herself. "I'll be back later."

Rest and relax he said to himself, as he closed his eyes, hearing the sound of the ocean through the open window. The air was perfect, somehow both warm and cool, covering and surrounding him like two strong arms. He felt his head resting against a strong, solid chest, felt the softness of a beard against his cheek. Dad?

"Jay," he said instead as he fell asleep.

Doyle told Jessie and all the townspeople who happened by that Peter Freeman, a football player for the San Francisco Forty-Niners, was in town, and right now he was lying in the infirmary. Yes, Nurse Walker was tending to him. No, I don't know what happened to him, if he's under attack by Satan or what. We'll have to pray for him, won't we? And yes, they'll make sure that he stays for the Father's Day picnic. Maybe he can even be a guest speaker at the Sunday morning service, or maybe the evening service.

No, I don't think he's saved. He doesn't have a fish on the back of his truck, that big garish red truck parked at the Saloon. And what about that? We all know what that means. And the "Saloon" sign brought him in, didn't it? Our Pastor was right, we have to bring in the sinners, and then save them. And you know how those sports figures are, all the drinking and drugs and everything else they're involved in, the girls, the lust, the pre-marital sex, all of that. And there's a lot of homosexuals in sports too, remember that one who "came out of the closet," as they say?

Oh yes, the football player had asked for a beer in the Saloon, Jessie told me that. So he *can't* be a Christian. Well, we'll just have to pray for his soul, won't we? We'll just have to see that he gets saved while he's here in La Sangre, won't we?

How long is he going to stay? I don't know, that's up to the Pastor, isn't it? But long enough to get saved, that's for sure. We'll just have to make sure of that, won't we? We'll just have to make sure that he doesn't leave La Sangre until he's saved.

TWELVE

Corey sat on a chair in the corner of the infirmary, watching Peter sleep. It was funny: when he first saw Peter in the Saloon he had the thrill of seeing a celebrity in person, close up, not far away like on TV or even at Candlestick Park. But now, being near him and talking to him and watching over him, per Nurse Walker's instructions, there was something else, as if he actually knew this man.

Peter awoke and saw Corey looking at him.

"Hi Pete," Corey said tentatively.

What was the kid's name? "Hi Corey," Peter said. He looked around. "What time is it?"

"Almost six."

"Six!" Peter jerked. ("We've got to get out of here," Jay had said.)

"Yeah Pete, you've been asleep for over three hours. Lillian told me to sit with you. She went out on an errand, she'll be right back."

Peter swung his legs around and sat on the cot. "Thanks."

"Sure."

"Where's the john?"

"Right there," Corey pointed to the open door of a half-bathroom.

Peter got up and Corey talked to him while he urinated. "A few minutes ago I tried the phone again. Mary said we still can't make any outgoing calls."

Peter splashed cold water on his face. "Well, I've got to get out of here." ("Before it's too late.")

Jay's voice, again. Peter grabbed a paper towel and looked at himself in the mirror. And once again, was it real? He thought he had resolved that it was a dream, nothing more. Suddenly he had an idea. Was this kid, Corey, in on this too?

In on what?

"Uh, Corey, I'd like to try the phone myself."

"Oh sure, it's up front."

Peter followed Corey through the empty store to the front counter, which had a heavy, black desk phone with no dial.

"Just pick it up," Corey told him, "it'll go through to Mary."

"Good afternoon, this is Mary," said a pleasant voice. "Praise the Lord!"

"Hello?" Peter said.

"Yes, with whom am I speaking? I show this call coming from the General Store."

"This is Pete Freeman."

"Oh, Mr. Freeman, yes. I'm sorry, I've been trying for a few hours to get an outside line, since Nurse Walker called for you, but for some reason I can't. This has happened before. It has something to do with the circuit between here and Santa Rosa."

"How about Fort Bragg? Can you reach an operator up there? Or Bodega Bay?"

"No, the problem seems to always be with our own circuit, leading out," she said smoothly. "As I said, this has happened before, we've had to wait for the phone company to come out and take care of it. They won't be able to do so over the weekend, not until Monday. And this is Father's Day weekend after all." She paused. "Is there anything else I can do for you?"

Peter wondered. Sure, why not? "Do you know anyone who can give me a ride into Santa Rosa?" He could buy the battery, bring it back himself, and just get out of Dodge. ("I got out of Dodge in a hurry," Jay had told him.)

"Hmmm...," Mary pondered, "No, no one that I can think of is going into Santa Rosa today. Everyone's getting ready for the Father's Day picnic tomorrow. All the supplies are in, there's no reason for anyone to drive into Santa Rosa. However, if you like, I can ask around and see if anyone who has a car—not too many people have cars here—can give you a ride. I can call you back at the General Store and let you know."

"Yeah," Peter said, defeated. "Thanks."

"Have a blessed day!"

Peter hung up and turned to Corey. "Do you know anyone I can ask for a ride into Santa Rosa? I'll pay them of course."

"Well," Corey considered. Just what's going on, he wondered not for the first time that day. He was used to being isolated in La Sangre, but he didn't really question it until this morning, when he talked with his mother on the bluff. He too, wanted to get out. And then the letter about his scholarship had arrived, and then Pete Freeman had arrived, his father yelling at him, cursing even...something was happening, Corey just didn't know what it was.

"Is there?" Pete repeated.

"Is there what? Oh, well, not too many people in La Sangre have cars."

"Yeah, the operator told me that."

"But Jessie's got one."

"Jessie?"

"The waitress in the saloon."

("The only thing I can offer you is Jack Daniels," she'd told Peter, "at my place.")

Peter shook his head. It was wrong. He'd been warned about her, and it didn't matter now, dream or no dream. He'd been warned about Jessie, and about La Sangre. "Is there anyone else?" Peter asked Corey.

"Well, my dad..uh, the Pastor..." Corey faltered ("you goddamn bastard!").

"He could give me a ride?" Peter asked.

"Well, he'd be the one to ask. Do you want me to do that?"

The Pastor, Peter wondered. What about that hasty exit back at the Saloon, half-dragging Corey and his mother out with him? Can anything happen in this town without the Pastor's control? ("He owns this whole damn town," Jessie had said. "He owns everything and everyone here except me, and some day I'm going to be the first and only one to tell him that his shit smells like everyone else's!")

"Do you?" Corey repeated.

"Do I what?'

"Do you want me to ask my father if someone can drive you into Santa Rosa?"

"No," Peter said warily. "You'd better not."

Good Peter. Be careful.

Doyle shut off the gas pumps at the La Sangre Last Chance Gas Station and Garage promptly at six, keeping an eye on the Saloon, waiting for the door to open and for Jessie to walk out. She was a godly woman, he said to himself, with a good, strong spirit. In a way, though, she reminded him of that little whore back in McCarthy, Texas. But perhaps that was only because of how she looked, a rather worldly way about her. Maybe if she wore clothes that were more...well, more *Christian*, less...less *worldly*, perhaps then she might be the woman that God has been preparing for him. He must continue to pray about it.

Doyle began to pray as he folded up and moved the "Last Chance Gas" sandwich sign into the office, and at that very moment the Saloon door opened and Jessie emerged. His spirit leaped—it was indeed an answer to his prayer. Jessie was to be his wife! All he had to do was discipline her, about what she wore for example, and then he would be ready to receive her.

He quickly locked the unleaded gas pumps. Unleaded! It still angered him. He missed the good old days of just regular and ethyl, like when he worked at the gas stations back in Texas, and then New Mexico, Utah, and Nevada. But two years ago, here in La Sangre, the California Department of Land, Air and Water Resources had required the old steel gas nozzles be refitted with the newer, rubber sealed ones "so that gas fumes won't leak into the air, and gas won't be spilled," they explained to him. Doyle belligerently told them he'd never spilled a drop of gas in his life.

Doyle had complained to the Pastor about the Commission's requirements; after all, they live right next to the ocean, the air is always clean, what difference could two pumps make? But the Pastor explained he could do nothing about it, that he had to pick his battles with the State. They were just fortunate, the Pastor reminded Doyle, that God had seen to it that their gas station had passed the underground storage tank test. As if, Doyle responded to the Pastor, a little gas leaking into the ground would hurt anything.

Pumps locked and shut off, office locked, Doyle brushed his hands on his white overalls—they needed washing, he'll have to ask one of the women to wash them for him—and hurried up the walkway.

"Praise the Lord, Sister Jessie!" he hailed her.

"Well praise the Lord, Brother Doyle!" Indeed. She'd hoped she would miss him. But she was, after all, leaving La Sangre tomorrow. She could do this performance one more time. "How are you Brother?"

"Well, the Lord is truly blessing me. Every day He blesses me. I take such joy in serving Him, working at the Garage, and He truly blesses me in return."

"Well you know Brother, the Bible says that each of us has our place in the body, and if we're each serving joyfully, then the blessings will truly come upon us, as they do to all of us here in La Sangre!"

"Amen! We are just so blessed to be living here!"

"Amen to that, Brother!" Jessie closed her eyes. Oh please.

"May I walk you home, Sister?" Doyle surprised himself at his boldness, and knew that it must be of the Lord. Yes, his prayer for a wife had truly been answered. But another thought crossed his mind: he knew she was leaving tomorrow, why did he wait until now to offer to escort her home? He brushed it away.

"Please do, Brother Doyle," Jessie nodded in what she was certain was overplayed modest consent. "I would enjoy your fellowship. I feel the Lord working through you in such a powerful way." This guy is so easy to fool, I can run the whole gamut. And since this is my last evening here, why don't I go for it and have a little fun?

Doyle again felt his spirit leap within him. "Yes," he said excitedly as they crossed the road together. "I do feel the Lord working through me. The Pastor has mentioned that very thing to me, and it gives me such joy, just to serve. And this very morning God gave me a message about someone who came into our town, a warning about an attack by Satan, and then the Pastor confirmed that message, and we united in a prayer of protection against this attack, and God gave us instructions on what to do. We truly are blessed to have such a man of God as our Pastor, as our protector and shepherd."

"Amen to that, Brother!" Jessie responded. Someone who came into town? Oh, probably that baseball...no, football player. Satan indeed.

But then, there was that other man with him, big man, red beard. Had Corey believed her lie that she didn't see him?

"Amen sister!" Doyle was excited as they reached the dirt road leading down to the homes. Doyle would walk Jessie to her door...and then what? Maybe she'll invite him in?

A pang of fear went through Doyle. Invite you in? For what Doyle?

"Yes," Jessie said, hoping Doyle wouldn't take her arm. Naw, no way would Doyle try something as forward as that. "Yes, the Pastor is such a righteous man, a holy man, and so knowledgeable of the Word. He is truly a good shepherd, leading and feeding the flock here in La Sangre. Yes," she looked over at the Satoris' two-story house on the north end of town, "yes, I just love that bastard!"

Doyle almost stopped walking, not sure if he heard right. "Uh...yes," he rallied, certain he was mistaken. "I just love that Pastor too."

Unnoticed, as usual, Lillian had watched the charade between Jessie and Doyle from the front window of the General Store as she closed up. Peter and Corey were seated on stools at the counter, in conversation. So, old Doyle finally got up the courage to walk Jessie home. Poor Jessie. For that matter poor Doyle. It's a good thing for him she's leaving tomorrow.

And why don't *you* leave, Lillian?

Because there's something I have to do first, Lillian said to herself.

Yes Lillian, what is that?

Peter Freeman. She had to talk to him.

About what?

About everything, Lillian told herself. I talked to Peter when he came to, after I gave him the ammonia inhalant. I checked his vitals, asked him questions, did my job as a nurse. And like the good nurse that I am, I was able to make a fair assessment of him. He's an upright man, straightforward and refreshingly honest.

Earlier in the day I also talked to Connie, or rather, she talked to me. Peter and Connie are both from Bakersfield, in the same high school class, the same age. I had wisely kept my mouth shut to Peter about Connie, and now I know why. ("How do those things happen," Connie had asked me, "when we don't even consider them? Are they allowed to happen? Are they *supposed* to happen?")

And what about that scene I witnessed outside the Saloon at lunch today, between Sal and Connie and Corey? They had exited the Saloon right after Peter had entered, and yes, he was alone. There was no sign of the stranger Peter had told me about when I was examining him.

Yes. I have to talk to Connie again, and then I have to talk to Peter.

Because Peter Freeman is Corey Satori's father.

Lillian froze in that knowledge, and then reversed the "Open" sign to "Closed." She got an idea and turned to Peter.

"Pete?"

He and Corey both turned to her.

"Pete, why don't you come over to my home for dinner?"

Peter looked at her, then at Corey.

"You too Corey," Lillian said.

"Sure!" Corey said happily, looking at Peter. "I'll just call my Mom, let her know I won't be home for dinner." He headed for the phone.

"No wait Corey," Lillian said. "I have to stop by your Mom's for a minute anyway. I'll tell her. You two go on ahead, I'll be there in about ten minutes."

"Can we get in?" Peter asked.

"City boy," Lillian teased him. "We don't lock our doors in La Sangre."

Lillian looked at Corey, then at Peter. Yes, it was unmistakable, they were father and son. No, she wouldn't be the one to tell them, but she'd make sure they found out, from Connie herself. In any case she wouldn't, couldn't, separate them this soon. They looked beautiful together, unaware, and yes, there was a love between them that they weren't aware of yet. Corey loved him as his football hero, and Peter liked, no loved him as an adoring kid. As a beautiful, trusting boy. This was something, Lillian was sure, that Peter needed at this point in his life. He was sent to La Sangre for a reason, and maybe that fantasy stranger was...an angel? It was possible, and scriptural.

"You know Pete, tomorrow's the Father's Day picnic," Corey said. "Good food. We can throw the football around."

Peter mulled it over. ("We've got to get out of here, Peter!") Short of hiking out in the dark—and he'd never make it to Santa Rosa—he didn't have a choice. Tomorrow should be soon enough...if he can get a ride. As far as spending the night, he had his overnight bag with him. He liked this kid, who seemed to be more than just a starstruck fan. ("It's not that I wanted a son so much," he'd told Jay, "but what I wanted was to somehow recreate myself, make a perfect and unblemished me, that I could love and accept.") He shook his head. Reality or unreality, whatever it is, he'll just go with the flow.

"Is that a no?" Lillian asked him.

"Oh no!" Peter said quickly. "I just...I hadn't thought of it. Yeah, I'd like to. I'd like a home-cooked meal." He found he wanted to spend some time with Lillian too. He liked her, felt comfortable with her. Around her and Corey, La Sangre felt..normal. Well, kind of.

Lillian smiled. "I'll throw something

together. I'm a good cook."

"Will I sleep here?" Peter regarded the cot in the back of the infirmary.

"No Pete," Corey said enthusiastically. "I've got two beds in the room I just moved into, above the garage. I share a bathroom with Doyle. It's got a shower."

Doyle. Well, he'd shared bathrooms and showers with hundreds of teammates over the years, some, especially linemen, as mean and crazy as Doyle seems to be. He can handle one more.

"Fine," Peter said.

THIRTEEN

Sal was waiting at the gate of the Owens' cottage when Doyle and Jessie arrived.

"Praise the Lord, Pastor!" Doyle greeted him, certain that the Pastor's presence was yet another sign that Jessie was to be his wife.

"Doyle," Sal nodded perfunctorily, and turned to Jessie. "Jessie, I'd like to speak to you about something."

"Well," Jessie looked over at Doyle, "I was just going to ask Doyle to come in so we could read the Bible and pray. But," she smiled sweetly at Doyle, "we can do that some other time, can't we?"

"But..." Doyle stumbled, "I thought you were leaving tomorrow."

"Maybe," she shrugged coyly, "maybe not. I might stay on."

Doyle's face showed a mixture of delight and fear, while Sal's jaw dropped.

Yes, Jessie thought smugly, the only thing more powerful, and more satisfying, than manipulating a man was manipulating two of them at the same time.

"Well..." Doyle saw the look between Jessie and the Pastor as his leave, "I'll see you in church tomorrow, Sister Jessie."

Jessie just nodded, keeping her eyes on the Pastor as Doyle walked off. As usual, she let the Pastor take the offense in what she knew would be their final confrontation, what she'd been preparing for.

"What was *that* all about?" Sal asked her, not disguising his irritation.

"What was *what* all about?" she responded simply. Strike One.

"Having prayer and Bible study with Doyle some time. You'd told me you were leaving Monday, after Father's Day."

"I didn't say I was leaving Monday. I said the Owens were returning Monday." Strike Two.

Sal closed his eyes. "So, are you going to leave when they get here?"

"Yes."

"Then why did you just say you might not leave?"

Jessie kept her eyes on Sal, steady, not blinking. "I'll explain." She let out a sigh and then, Sal could see, unmistakably and surprisingly, she dropped her guard. That guard she'd kept up against him, and La Sangre, for nine months. "Actually Pastor, I have a lot of explaining to do."

Her nasty, manipulative tone was suddenly gone, and she had become something else, something Sal had never seen. This wasn't the wanton flirt with the whorey attitude she'd had with him earlier that day, nor was it the pious Christian woman she played...yes, *played*...at church and in Bible study. This was a new Jessie that was...real. Vulnerable. Soft.

"Pastor...Sal, I really do need to explain some things. I know I've been reserved...no, cold, even nasty around you, all this time I've been in La Sangre. But there's been a reason for it. It's not an excuse for my bad behavior, and I hope you'll forgive me for that, but there's a reason nonetheless, and I'd like to explain it to you." She paused effectively. "No, I *need* to explain it to you."

"Yes," Sal nodded. At first he thought he was automatically going into his compassionate Pastor's mode. But no, it was different. His tone was lower, more natural to himself. He was being...who *was* this man? This man inside of me. Where has he been?

"Why don't you come on in?" She glanced around at the other homes. "We can talk inside." Her eyes had become as soft as her tone.

Yes, Sal knew. This was the real Jessie. It's true that she had never before sought him for counsel, and of course his attempts to reach her had been thwarted. But since she was leaving La

Sangre, maybe it was easier now for her to talk to him, to confess. She would confess her sins, and it was his job, as Pastor, to listen. Indeed, hers was the body he saw this morning on the rocks at the bottom of the cliff, broken and bloody. And it was his job to bring her to the Lord, lovingly. And yet, it wasn't his automatic Pastor mode that was doing this, it was a new—or old—Salvatore Satori. Where has he been?

Jessie turned and walked up the path to the house. She opened the screen door and unlocked the front door. Nobody in La Sangre locked their doors, Sal noted. But then, this was the Owens' property, not Jessie's. She probably felt responsible.

Sal had never been inside the Owens' cottage, and they had always made it clear they weren't interested in anything that La Sangre represented or had to offer. With Jessie staying here he always remained outside, in the front yard, if he had to talk to her about something, such as work at the Saloon. But now he realized that all this time, the entire year, he had in fact wanted to go inside, to be with Jessie. He needed to talk with...no, needed to *be with* Jessie, as much as she, he was now sure, needed to be with him.

Sal watched her through the screen door as she leaned against the arm of an easy chair and slipped her shoes off.

"Come on in, Sal," Jessie said softly.

I will not shirk my duty, Sal tried to tell himself, I am the Pastor of La Sangre. But now his old familiar sense of power was diminishing, and a need was taking its place. A need to be needed, as a man. It caused his breathing to become deeper, his lungs filling up with the sea air, and then pushing it outwards. It felt so good to breathe freely like this; had the sea air ever tasted so good? His heartbeat accelerated, blood pumping forcefully through him, causing a wave of heat beginning at his heartcenter and spreading out through his chest, into his arms, and down into this thighs. Had this feeling, this need, been here all this time?

"Come on in, Sal," Jessie said again.

For the first time that he could remember, Sal stopped thinking. Gratefully, joyfully, he stopped thinking, stopped planning, stopped controlling. Relieved of his responsibility, of his duty, he walked up the path and opened the screen door and went inside. Jessie closed and locked the front door behind them.

Thirty minutes later Sal lay naked on the kitchen floor. It had started quickly, automatically, a natural flow of events right after Jessie had shut and locked the door. Wordlessly Sal had walked into the bedroom, undressed and got on the bed. Jessie followed as soon as she lowered the blinds throughout the cottage. She

came into the bedroom and Sal watched her
undress. She unzipped and stepped out of her
waitress uniform. As Sal had long noticed, she
wasn't wearing a bra, just a tee-shirt to prevent
her nipples from being seen through the uniform. She removed the shirt and lowered her
panties.

What a wonder, a miracle, a woman's body
is. A further wonder was that Jessie looked better nude than she did with clothes on, natural
and beautiful. She had a woman's body, not as
a man thought it should be, but as a woman's
body should be. Her breasts were small and
adequate, serving the purpose for which they
were intended, for an infant and for a man. Her
stomach wasn't flat, it had a natural mound to
it, with just a faint trace of blonde hair from her
naval downward. When she had raised her arms
to take her tee-shirt off, he saw another faint
trace of underarm hair, light and wispy. She was
a woman. She could nurture him, take care of
him...save him.

"Nice body," Jessie said as she joined Sal on
the bed. It took him a few seconds to realize she
was talking about his own.

The first round on the bed had begun and
ended quickly, Sal muffling his own cry, his eyes
wet. "That was good," was all he could finally
say.

"*Very* good," Jessie whispered, her head

resting on his shoulder. "Rest now."

But Sal rallied after just a few minutes.

"Well, I didn't know you had it in you," Jessie had laughed softly.

"Neither did I," Sal had whispered huskily as they resumed the...whatever it was. Was it love-making? He didn't know and didn't care, but it was, simply, good. Perfect in fact.

"Hey," Jessie had said after ten minutes on the bed, "did you ever make it under a table?"

"No," Sal chuckled, as if there could be another answer to that question.

"Neither have I," Jessie lied. "Come on."

He had followed her into the kitchen and they pulled the four chairs away from the oval wooden table.

"Ow!" Sal yipped at one point under the table.

"Mind your head!" Jessie quipped.

Second rounds are always the best, Sal realized for the first time in his life. They're longer, more exciting, more satisfying. "Ow!" he said again.

"The earth shook, and the table moved!" Jessie laughed, and Sal joined her in the laughter.

By this time Jessie was letting Sal take the lead. "Come on," he said after ten minutes under the table. "There's something I've always wanted to do."

He got out from under the table, took her by

the hand to pull her out and up, put his hands on her waist, and effortlessly hoisted her up onto the kitchen counter.

"Why Grandpa, what strong arms you have!" she said playfully. It wasn't a false compliment, Sal knew. He looked around the kitchen. In the corner, perfectly (again), was a step-stool, just the right height for his short legs. He placed it on the floor between Jessie's legs and stepped up on it; the perfect height, the perfect complement of a man and woman's bodies.

After another ten minutes of increasing speed and intensity they both gasped, then held their positions for a moment, clutching each other. It was better than the first time, almost frightening in its intensity. This indeed was heaven. Sal slowly bent forward, placing his nose into the nape of her neck. The softness, the warmth, the smell. Her hands stroked his hair. It was perfect.

After a minute, Sal let himself down off the stool and onto the kitchen floor. He lay there, happily exhausted, his head clear. Life was simple. Why hadn't he realized that before, not wait until he was 38 years old? What a fool he'd been all these years. A stupid, angry fool.

Jessie lowered herself from the counter and went into the bedroom.

"Where are you going?" Sal asked from the floor, hating to see her go.

"Be right back!" she promised.

And now he was lying on the kitchen floor. It was clean and even comfortable. He could stay like this forever. There was nothing else at that moment, nothing else existed. Not La Sangre, not church, not Connie or Corey...not even... what was it that had bothered him so much this morning? Something from the south? Whatever it was, not even that.

Too bad Jessie was leaving tomorrow. Well, they could meet somewhere, have this again, in Santa Rosa maybe. No, too close to home. Okay, further away then. Like a nice hotel room in San Francisco where nobody would know them. Yes, that's it. He could fabricate a church meeting there. It wouldn't be lying, because his district often had church meetings in San Francisco. He could meet with Jessie after any such meeting, then it definitely wouldn't be lying. That would be perfect. But he'd have a hard time sitting through those boring meetings, wanting to get to Jessie. Maybe he'd see her before the meeting instead. Before and after. No, he couldn't see her before the meeting; his content, his smile, how he felt right now, loved, he wouldn't be able to disguise it. Yes, after the meeting was better. And the anticipation, days before, how wonderful that would be.

Jessie came back into the kitchen wearing a terrycloth bathrobe and sat in a kitchen chair.

Sal was sorry she'd covered that wonderful

body, still he smiled up at her.

Then he froze.

She was staring at him. Victorious. Smug. It was the old Jessie, as if it had been inside all the time, waiting to re-emerge. The Jessie he'd just been with, had sex with, she had been performing for him, and it was...

Perfect.

"To answer your earlier question, Pastor," she said dryly in her old Jessie tone, as if nothing had happened since they were standing in the front yard, "I *am* leaving tomorrow. Right after the Father's Day picnic."

The Father's Day picnic. He suddenly remembered where he was. La Sangre.

Sal turned away, unable to look at her. He had kept his eyes on hers throughout the last 30 minutes, going deep into her limpid eyes. But what color were they? He couldn't remember. All he could remember was that it had been wonderful, 30 minutes of not thinking, of just letting something happen and riding it out like an ocean wave, feeling its power and freedom, without questioning it.

And now, the world that he had forgotten came back, flooding him like pieces of a jigsaw puzzle dropping from the ceiling onto the floor, on top of and around him. The pieces were falling haphazardly, some of them upside down. And none of them fit.

"Ah yes," Jessie observed Sal with experience. "The crashdown."

"Crashdown," Sal repeated weakly.

"Yes darling, the crashdown. Married men get it real bad, pastors and priests even more so. But don't worry Sal, it gets easier each time. Like alcohol, it tastes so bad when you experimentally sip it as a child, or try a cigarette, and then you eventually develop a taste for it, and it doesn't hurt anymore."

So this is hell, Sal knew. He had to go there, didn't he?

He couldn't move from the floor. He could almost feel those pieces of the puzzle on him and around him, used and soggy, jagged pieces of this insane world's giant jigsaw puzzle.

Yes, this is hell, Sal. What she calls the crashdown. The incredible high, and then the crash. And once this empty and hellish crash is over, you'll be back for more. You know you will.

"Why?" he asked her helplessly, not looking at her

"Why what Sal?"

"Why did you do it?" he asked.

"Why? Because I can Sal. Because I *can*."

"But...why me?"

"Oh Sal, the Owens told me all about you, and I was intrigued, then saw it as a challenge. And I can resist anything but a challenge. Sal, consider it a compliment; after all it took nine months with you. With the others it usually takes just nine days."

Sickened and weak, Sal got up from the floor. He avoided Jessie's triumphant gaze and went into the bedroom to retrieve his clothes. He noticed that all of the windows in the cottage were covered, something he hadn't even thought about during the half hour of wonderful madness. At least she had done that. She had lowered the blinds when all he could think about was touching her.

Jessie followed him into the bedroom and watched him dress. "Sal, it took me a lifetime to understand something, and you need to know this: we're not sinners because we sin. We *sin* because we're *sinners*. Besides, our sins keep us humble. So you see, they serve a purpose. Just remember that, Sal, and stop *thinking* so damned much, and you'll be fine."

Sal considered what she said as he pulled on his pants. Is that true? It made sense, but was it true? No, it can't be that way. Not for him.

"Thinking again?" Jessie chuckled in her final triumph. "Ah yes, the old Pastor Salvatore Satori is back." She walked into the bathroom and began to run the water in the sink. "You'll forgive me if I don't offer you a shower. Oh by the way, from now on you can think about our wild fucking under the table the next time you say the blessing before a meal."

FOURTEEN

Connie stood on the deck, watching the sun finally touch the horizon of the Pacific Ocean. The seagulls had long quieted down. It's about time, she thought wryly, that this day was over. She couldn't believe that it was the same day that had seen her final good-bye to her son, Sal's disgusting outburst in the Saloon, the arrival of Peter, her talk with Lillian.

Had Peter recognized her in the Saloon? She didn't think so. It was just seconds in the Saloon and she'd changed so much since Bakersfield. But he hadn't changed at all. More body mass perhaps, more mature face, but he was the same beautiful young man she'd known all those years ago.

"Known," she smiled with irony. That was the word all right. Did Sal suspect? (Where *was* Sal anyway? Dinner was ready.) He must suspect something, or else why would he have reacted so violently in the Saloon? ("Shutup, you goddamn bastard!") But how could he suspect? Was God indeed speaking to people in La Sangre as directly as they liked to believe? Or were they just replacing their own agendas, imaginations, and unwarranted suspicions with "God revealed to me that fill-in-the-blank."

This is what she'd wanted to talk, finally talk, to Sal about in the kitchen, only he wanted to pray instead. She'd long believed that he hid behind prayer rather than use it to communicate with God. She and Sal had never really communicated with each other. Given that, could they really communicate with God? Like the Bible says, if you don't really love people, you can't really love God.

This afternoon in the kitchen, Connie faced the fact that she and Sal had become amusement park operators, and the people of La Sangre mindlessly went along for the religious ride. A few, like Lillian, fought against it...or left town.

She couldn't stand it if Lillian left. That would force Connie to proceed with moving back to Bakersfield. Unless...unless she can get Sal to communicate with her. She gripped the railing of the deck with both hands.

"Father in heaven," she prayed out loud, "I can't reach Sal, and maybe it's too late for me to do so. But I know You can. Please let Sal see the Truth, Your Truth, not the fears and doubts that may cloud his, or my, faith. Let Sal deal with the Truth as You see fit, not as he or I may be led by our own inadequacies and insecurities."

She watched the round slice of orange sun sink slowly into the ocean, and waited for an answer.

"Connie?"

She jumped.

"I'm sorry Connie," Lillian said. "I didn't mean to surprise you."

"That's all right," Connie let out a breath. "I was praying."

Lillian sighed. "That's something I haven't been doing enough of. I think I've been just riding on God's grace."

"But sometimes that's enough, sometimes not. It's hard to be smart that way."

Lillian remembered something she'd heard as a child, in the La Sangre Christian Church from their wonderful, old, long-time Pastor, who had died and whom Sal had replaced: If you knew the difference between man's responsibility and God's will, you *would* be God.

The two women were silent for a moment, in their own considerations.

"Well," Lillian broke the silence, "I just stopped by to tell you that Corey's going to have dinner at my place. With Peter. It was my idea. Corey hated to see Peter leave, so...I'm just delaying it. He still can't drive his truck, and Mary says the phone line is still down. I hope you don't mind."

"No, that's fine," Connie nodded, realizing

that she was still gripping the railing of the deck. She was glad Corey and Peter were together. She released her grip. "Lillian, we have a private line in the house."

"What? You do? I never knew that."

"I only discovered it by accident. Sal didn't want anyone to know, not even me and Corey. He wanted people to think he's just like them, open and guileless, one of the 'common people,' with Mary vigilante to his calls as well as everyone else's."

Does his need for control never end? Lillian wondered. He's as indomitable in this town as...

Yes, as God.

Lillian shook her head, sickened. "Connie, let's use that line to call out, a tow truck, anyone outside of here."

"He keeps it locked up. Corey and I have to go through Mary."

Well, he may be the god of La Sangre, Lillian thought with disgust, but not God of the Truth. "Connie, you don't have to answer this if you don't want to."

Connie braced herself. "Go ahead Lillian."

"Peter is Corey's father, isn't he?"

It's about time. Connie nodded. She was tired of all this. "Do they know?"

"No."

"Are you sure?"

"Yes. Corey is very taken by Peter, but I think

only because of football. Peter is a big celebrity you know."

Connie nodded. "Corey and Sal would watch him play on TV, they'd cheer whenever he made a run, scored a touchdown. They both thought he was the best running back the Forty-Niners had."

"And you watched him play too?"

"Of course, but I always managed to stand or sit behind them, so they couldn't see my reaction."

"Which was?"

Connie turned to Lillian. No, she couldn't stand it if Lillian left La Sangre. "Oh Lillian, he was just as beautiful on that football field as he was in high school, even more so, if that's possible. Sal and Corey must have suspected something, somehow, on some level. I've never told Sal who Corey's father is, only my parents know. But Sal must know on that same level that I believe Corey and Peter know, or else why would Sal act the way he did today? And how did *you* know?"

"Just from what you told me," Lillian said. "He's from Bakersfield, your age." But that wasn't enough, Lillian realized. How *did* I know? It was more than a hunch, or a woman's intuition. Had God revealed it to me? Just like God told me this morning that something was going to happen this weekend in La Sangre? "Connie, did Peter recognize you in the Saloon?"

Connie shook her head. "He couldn't have. I told you, I was a plain jane then. Not too many people recognize me from that time. After I had Corey I developed breasts, hips, my face filled out. I add blonde coloring to my mousy brown hair. Besides, Peter didn't even look at me in the Saloon today."

Connie looked out at the ocean, which held the final rays of the sun. It's the ocean, she thought, that has final say over when the light is gone, not the sun. Then the ocean itself darkens and reveals its secrets, its wisdom of the day. The ocean, God, is indeed dispensing the truth and making me brave.

"Growing up," Connie told Lillian, "especially in school but even in church, people looked through me. I was invisible. But Peter always looked at me whenever he saw me, on the bus, in the hallways. He'd see right into my eyes, with those beautiful blue eyes of his. I wasn't invisible to him."

Lillian waited a moment. "Tell me Connie," she finally said.

"Beginning in grade school, first grade in fact, I was unanimously chosen as the 'cooty girl.' They called me Connie-Cooty? Remember that? 'Don't touch her, she's got cooties!' And Peter was so popular, so beautiful and athletic, but in our first, second and third grade classes that we shared he was always nice to me. One time he was running for the school bus, late—oh could he run—and when he got on, there were no seats left, except next to me. And he didn't hesitate, he just sat down, and said 'Hi Connie.' Some of his friends started taunting him, 'Hey Pete, you're going to get cooties sitting next to her!' He turned around and told them to shut-up, and they did." Tears were streaming down Connie's face by this time. "Years later, at a high school dance, he walked up to me and asked me to dance."

Lillian wanted to say "That's incredible," but didn't want Connie to take it the wrong way. "What was the song?" she asked instead.

"'When A Man Loves A Woman.'"

"That's incredible," Lillian said.

"I'm sure the kids were staring at us, wondering why the most popular boy in school would ask me to dance, but I didn't care. For three whole minutes nothing else mattered."

They were quiet for a moment, the tune to "When A Man Loves A Woman" nearly audible to them both.

"Oh Lillian, he was so beautiful, so open. Corey is just like him."

"They don't look alike," Lillian said. "Corey seems to favor you."

"The face, yes, but don't you see the way they're both built, the way they walk? The sleekness, the grace, the light step, like a gazelle. Corey always loved to run, you know that. He'd take those long runs up and down Route 1. I used to worry about cars hitting him, but there was no way I was going to stop him. I loved to watch him run."

Lillian nodded. "So how did it...happen?"

"I was still unpopular in junior high and high school, even though the 'cooty' taunts stopped. Peter was still nice to me. I couldn't believe it when he asked me out, just before graduation, because he was going with one of the most popular girls in the school, one of the cheerleaders. So I didn't understand, but I accepted his invitation. Can you imagine the torment I had trying to make myself look nice? I wore my best church dress." She gave a mild laugh, her eyes and cheeks still moist. "I even thought about stuffing my bra, can you believe that?"

"I did," Lillian chuckled. "I think all of us ironing boards did."

"Well I thought about it but I didn't, only because I knew Peter wouldn't care. I actually knew that."

"So, what happened?"

"My parents were so happy that I had a date. And they knew who Peter was, he was in the Bakersfield newspaper all the time due to football. College scouts were watching him at the games. And he'd gotten a scholarship from

UCLA by that time."

"Weren't your parents suspicious of Peter's... motives?"

"Yes, and they asked me if I knew what his intentions were. Typical parents-of-a-teenager stuff. I just told them that we were going to a movie or something. But we just went driving, and I knew he just wanted to talk, which was fine."

"Gee Connie, I feel like a teenage girl asking this, but...what did he drive?"

Connie laughed. "One of his Dad's company pickups. We drove around with 'Lawrence Freeman Produce' on the doors. Peter apologized for it, said his father didn't want him to have his own car yet, not until he got into college. But I liked that company truck, it felt so big and masculine around me. So we talked, and I knew that was the reason he asked me out, but I didn't care. Peter knew that I would listen, and he must have known that I liked him."

"I don't know," Lillian said. "Boys, men, can be pretty dumb."

"That's true, but I could tell he didn't really have anyone else he could talk to, not even his sisters, they were too young, and certainly none of his friends. He told me his friends just wanted him to act cool, to be popular...and he said his girlfriend, the cheerleader, was that way. She didn't listen to anyone but herself, and he was glad we were graduating so he could get away from her. But, he told me, he didn't want to break up with her directly, he didn't want to hurt her. He couldn't be himself around her, whatever or whoever 'he' was."

"That kind of behavior is atypical for a high school star," Lillian commented. "No one like that even looked at me in high school."

In another shared silence, both women thought what a shame it was they waited this long to become friends.

"So Peter talked," Connie went on, "mostly about his father, who thought Peter should be more like him. Work hard, make lots of money. The football thing was fine, his father told him, and yes it had supplied Peter with a full scholarship at UCLA, but he'll have to major in business administration and then come back to Bakersfield to run the company. The football thing won't last forever, he told Peter. His father exerted so much *control* over him; even making him use the company truck to get around in was some kind of not-so-subtle message."

"Well, I guess Peter proved his father wrong, didn't he?"

"I guess. But Lillian, when I saw him today, the minute I saw him, saw his face...I could tell he was lost. He looked the same way he did that night in Bakersfield. Lost."

"So that night the two of you...talked," Lillian

gently prompted Connie.

"He pulled the truck over, onto one of the farming roads outside of town somewhere. He said his father dominated him, overpowered him, stifling his growth, at least his emotional growth. He actually told Peter 'If you're such a hot shot football player, then why are you so goddamn sensitive?'"

"Ouch," Lillian said. That's almost as bad as "goddamn bastard," she didn't add.

"And he *was* sensitive, which was unusual for someone so 'popular.' In those days, if you were popular in high school you didn't have to question anything else in life, you just went along. But Peter questioned it. And..." Connie turned away from Lillian to the ocean, not ashamed, but in way of keeping the memory as her own. "And I gave myself to him. Like I told you earlier, neither of us expected it, and it wasn't why he asked me out. It just happened, and it was beautiful." She turned back to Lillian. "I don't know if I should be sorry for what I did, but I'm not."

Lillian looked at Connie. Beautiful, soft, pleasant Connie. This was no "Pastor's wife," this was a real woman. No, Lillian thought to herself, you don't have to be sorry. There's nothing to be sorry for.

Connie sighed and turned back to the ocean and its final light. "And you know the rest of the story."

"What about your parents? Didn't they suspect that Peter just..."

"Oh I told them exactly how it happened, why it happened, and that I knew there was no relationship to pursue. I begged them not to call him or his parents, not for money, not for anything."

"And they didn't?"

"No. It's a miracle now that I think of it. They always trusted my judgment; I was the good, sensible girl, and they respected that. But I think the big surprise, to them and to me, was that Peter should...find me attractive. It gave me a lot to live for, and at times I wanted to shout it from the rooftops of Bakersfield, that 'Connie Cooty' had gotten her revenge."

Lillian smiled at her. "Good for you, Connie." Both women watched the darkening ocean for a few minutes, until Lillian spoke.

"You said Sal follows football, followed Peter in particular. Does he know that you went to the same high school as Peter, the same class?"

"Yes, and he asked me once if I'd known him. I just said he was popular and I wasn't. Besides, I still looked like Connie-Cooty when Sal met me, there was no way he'd put me together with Peter. No one in Bakersfield would have thought it possible. So Sal let it go at that."

Lillian waited a respectable minute. "Are you going to tell Corey?"

"Yes, when he turns 18."

"Why then?"

"I don't know, maybe the legality of it. Peter will know that I've never wanted anything from him, rich as he probably is."

"And what about telling Sal?"

"I have to, but I sure don't want to. I don't want to hurt Sal any more than I have. He's gone through enough, with me and Corey practically excluding him from our closeness. He doesn't deserve to be destroyed any more."

Sal stood at the hairpin turn on Route 1 south of La Sangre, where he had sat that morning. He couldn't go back home, not after what he did.

("Think about our wild fucking under the table the next time you say the blessing before a meal.")

No Sal, you can't go back home, back to La Sangre. What will you do there? Be the head of your family? Preach from the pulpit, counsel people in your smug, arrogant way? Allow people to believe that you're the sinless leader of their town, the only one in town who has a firm understanding of God, an encyclopedic knowledge of the Bible?

And what about the things you do? You make every decision in town. Every phone call, practically every conversation, goes through you. You give people little jobs with all of the responsibility but none of the authority. And when anyone questions you, you just raise your voice and glare at them, knowing they'll back down every time. And if they don't back down, you just add them to your list of enemies. Didn't you do that with the Owens, with their polite refusal to attend your church? And haven't you let little remarks slip like "We all have to pray for the Owens," not-so-subtly implying that they're agnostics, or worse, atheists?

You walk proudly through town, Sal, up and down Highway 1, reveling in your control. And if something happens beyond your control, you know just how to deal with it. Right?

Sal held his breath, wanting the voice to stop, yet somehow needing to hear all it had to say. He had it coming.

You know just how to deal with it, don't you Sal? Like having your lackey pump-jockey steal Pete Freeman's battery? Yes, the football player, Sal. Just what is it, what is it about him that sets you off?

'GOD HELP ME!" Sal screamed. And he waited.

The ocean kept crashing against the rocks below.

"ARE YOU THERE?"

Don't worry Sal. Don't worry, God forgives all things, you know that. He'll forgive you for the way you've behaved in this town, the control,

GARY KYRIAZI

the judgment, the arrogance, the pride. He'll forgive you for stealing. And...the voice paused for emphasis. Sal gritted his teeth.

And He'll forgive you for the adultery you just committed.

It was pure sarcasm. Triumphant, joyful, reveling in Sal's destruction.

"GOD!" Sal screamed.

The ocean just crashed against the rocks, mocking him. There was enough light left, just a slice of the sun setting over the ocean, creating a sharp contrast between the ocean and the cliff, making dark shadows on the jagged edges of the rocks below. The salt water was hitting them, complementing them and giving them power.

As a last attempt, Sal grabbed onto that thought, the ocean and its power. Was it just this morning he had considered that? Yes, during his walk this morning, he realized that he was at one with the ocean: strong and unafraid in the knowledge that any trouble, any evil, that came into his town would be dashed against the rocks at the bottom of the cliff, broken and bloody, and then gently and lovingly brought to the Lord.

"GOD! IS THAT WHAT YOU WANT? ME, DOWN THERE?"

The crashing, the subsiding, the crashing again. Like God's heartbeat. Sal's own heartbeat was in perfect time with that of the ocean's. Yes, he was still at one with the ocean.

Sal, God can forgive anything. Suicide is not the unforgivable sin, you know that. Nowhere does it state that the suicides will not find their place in heaven.

"GOD, YOU HAVE TO ANSWER ME!"

The ocean crashing against the rocks.

"TELL ME SOMETHING! ANYTHING!"

It was Sal's last attempt to reach God. He waited.

Go ahead Sal. Jump. You'll land on the rocks below, broken and bloody, and then brought lovingly to the Lord.

"HELP ME GOD!" Sal cried, in the primeval scream of mankind.

He waited again.

Nothing.

And no answer is the same as an answer.

Sal was defeated.

He stepped over the guard rail.

FIFTEEN

J essie got out of the shower and stood briefly in front of the mirror. She was lucky with her fine features and very light, fine hair: she didn't have to wear makeup, didn't need to shave, and consequently any time she had to spend in front of the mirror was mercifully brief. She checked that her short, simple haircut was neat; her hair was the only thing about her that required any time to look at herself, or at least to look at her own reflection.

She put on her cotton nightgown; she had expected that the spring would bring warmer weather, even on the coast, but it was still cold. And that ocean. It was cold, harsh, and she didn't like it. She didn't like the sound it made. And those goddamn seagulls, the way they seemed to taunt her.

But she'd done her job. She'd taken the Pastor down, destroyed him, on her last night in La Sangre, just as she'd planned. That poor fool didn't know that over the last nine months every thing she'd said, every posture, every attitude she struck, was designed to trap him. If she wanted to she could have gotten him earlier, but she found by this time in her life that the hunt was as exciting, even more so, than the capture. So she waited the full nine months, and capture him she did. And damned good it was.

No, not the sex. The sex was never good. It worked, that's all. It had always worked. Since she was eight years old, when she was taught how to make it work for her.

Jessie had some fruit, yogurt, and cheese for dinner, cleaned up the kitchen, and checked to make sure the front door was locked. She'd locked it after the Pastor had left, but she wanted to make sure. You never can tell.

She went into the bedroom and lit a candle. She liked sleeping by candlelight; she liked the caress of the flame, its gentle flicker, the shadows it created. She never slept without it. It kept her from the dark. That horrible darkness. She'd hated the dark for as long as she could remember. She wasn't afraid of it, she just hated it. She hated what it would bring, lying in her bed in her father's home.

Jessie got into bed and watched the movement of the candle. Yes, she'd completed her task today, but it still wasn't enough, not this time. She didn't feel satisfied like she usually did. There was something else she had to do before she left La Sangre tomorrow, on Father's

Day. Maybe it'll come to her in the morning, after that taste of death that's called sleep.

"Tired?" Lillian watched Peter stifle a yawn across the table.

"I'm sorry," he smiled, embarrassed. "No, I shouldn't be. I took a long nap. I'm enjoying this." Indeed, the good dinner, Lillian's cozy cottage, her kindness and wit, and Corey's youthful enthusiasm had warmed Peter. He was in no hurry to leave.

"You boys have enough to eat?"

"I'm good," Peter said.

"Me too," Corey agreed.

"Come on boy," Peter told him, "have that last bit of spaghetti."

Corey smiled and took it.

"So," Peter said to Corey while he ate, "we've been talking about me and football, you haven't said what your plans are now that you've graduated. You got the scholarship. Do you want to be a pastor like your Dad?"

Lillian lowered her eyes. Corey's real father asking him if he wanted to be a pastor like his Dad. It was ironic and yet wonderful, watching father and son get to know each other. It was better, she decided, that they didn't know they were father and son. They could get to know each other without any expectations on either side. They were free to be who they were.

"A pastor like my Dad?" Corey chewed and thought. "I don't know. I just don't know what I want, period. You knew what you wanted after high school, didn't you Pete?"

Peter frowned, remembering that evening in Bakersfield with Connie O'Hara, an evening he'd never forgotten. That was what he'd wanted: the peace that he'd felt that night. Had he ever really felt that peace since then? "No, not really," he said, answering Corey's question. "As far as school and career, I didn't know what I wanted. But see, that was all set up for me, the football scholarship, four years at UCLA, and then I got drafted by the Forty-Niners. I guess," Peter considered, "I guess I just went along with it. Sure I had the talent, I knew that, and I worked hard. But it was easy, because I didn't have to make a decision." He turned to Lillian. "So 'Nurse Walker,' did you know what you wanted?"

Lillian smiled. Like Peter, she felt restful and content. She couldn't remember the last time she'd cooked for a man. It was a forgotten pleasure. "Did I know what I wanted when I graduated?" she repeated. Yes, it was time to talk about it. She looked at Corey. "Well, young man, I think you're old enough to hear this."

Peter leaned back in his chair to listen and, endearingly Lillian noticed, Corey copied his posture.

"Well, I was raised here, like Corey was. And

all I could think of was 'How am I going to get out of La Sangre?' The town was different then, it was just a plain old town. Everyone knew each other, but it wasn't as, well, constricted as it is now." She sighed. "My folks were both killed in a boating accident out of Bodega Bay when I was 17. It was tragic for me of course, but it also left me with complete freedom to do what I wanted. There was some insurance money, this cottage was paid off, and I'd always been independent, being an only child, like you" she smiled at Corey. "So the court approved that I could stay with a neighbor and family friend while I graduated from Santa Rosa High School. Then I decided to leave town and go to nursing school. I figured that if I became an RN I'd have even more freedom; job security and the ability to work anywhere I wanted. So I went north."

"Where up north?" Peter asked. ("As long as it's anywhere north, I'm good," Jay had told him.)

"Seattle. This was in 1960, and the World's Fair was being planned. I thought it would be exciting—and I was craving excitement—to be in the World's Fair city. So I rented out the cottage, took the bus to Seattle, rented a room, enrolled in nursing school, and worked part time so I wouldn't burn through the insurance money. And yes, it was exciting, especially watching the Space Needle get higher every day, to its

600-foot height. I thought it was the most beautiful thing I'd ever seen, and being there, at 18 years old, it represented my own life being built.

"When the Fair started in '62 I took a part time job working at the fairgrounds, in the amusement section. I wanted to work there rather than in the exhibits because the idea of the carnival, the traveling show, was yet more excitement for me. I worked the ticket booth for the Wild Mouse, that roller coaster where the little car goes around those hair-pin turns."

"I rode that at the fair in Santa Rosa," Corey said. "I thought that little car was going to fly off the track!"

Lillian smiled. "That's what I liked about it. 'Flying off the track,' as you say. I became friendly with one of the operators, about ten years older than I who'd been working carnivals since he was a teenager. He'd dropped out of school to join the carnival. Matthew—that was his name, he called himself Matt but I called him Matthew—he seemed to me the embodiment of the freedom and excitement that I loved. Working the World's Fair was the longest gig he'd had in one place since he was sixteen, and he'd tell me about his life on the road with the carnival, where they went, the different towns he got to know. We became...'involved' is the right word I think," she gave Corey a glance, "and I believed...no, I fantasized, that he'd take me away with him. I was skinny and plain, tall and flat-chested, but Matthew didn't seem to mind. He chose me, and that was all that mattered. I was certain he loved me." She paused and considered. "Well, that he *liked* me anyway."

"I like you Lillian," Peter said simply.

"Me too!" Corey echoed.

"Well, thank you boys. Everyone likes me. It's a quality—gift—that I never really appreciated until," she paused, thoughtful, "until this weekend."

Lillian stopped while the three of them looked at each other: what *was* it about this weekend? They all felt it.

"Well," Lillian broke the silence, "each night after the fair closed Matthew and I would go down to the waterfront bars and drink beer together. We danced to the jukebox. That song 'Johnny Angel' was 'our song.' Matthew thought it was silly but he humored me. And I'd sit on the bar stool and watch him shoot pool. More than once he'd get into a fight, usually over a pool game. One time it was a pretty bad fight, and I took him home and cared for him, cleaned up his cuts and bruises. I was happy." Lillian paused, surprised that the memory of it all wasn't painful. She wasn't sorry. ("I don't know if I should be sorry for what I did, but I'm not," Connie had said.)

Lillian started to go on with the story but

stopped. Yes, it was painful after all.

"So," Peter ventured, "what happened?"

Lillian looked down at the table. "I got pregnant, and Matthew told me that I couldn't go on the road with him with a baby. Of course in those days it was illegal, and there was no way I'd ask one of the other nurses for information, they gossip. So a girl at one of the bars told me of someone at the waterfront that could take care of the, uh, 'problem.' An upstairs room...dark and musty...cold, damp...newspapers spread over the floor..."

She stopped. Peter was looking at her with compassion. It happened a lot with NFL girlfriends. It had become legal ten years after Lillian's experience, and while Peter was fortunate it didn't happen to him and Kristi, he he had observed plenty of denied trauma, from the women, and surprisingly from some of the men.

Corey followed Peter's cue and watched Lillian, waiting for her to speak.

Lillian shook her head; yes, it was painful even now to think about it. "Well, the fair was over just a few weeks later, and Matthew left without telling me. He didn't come for me at my room like he said he would. I waited, suitcase packed, then suddenly I got scared and ran to the fairgrounds. I didn't even wait to take the monorail that went from downtown to the fair. I ran all the way. They were dismantling the Wild

Mouse as I got there, it was halfway down, those hairpin turns disconnected and stacked up like skeletal parts ready to be shipped. I remember thinking incoherently that disconnected like that, those cars would indeed fly off the track." She paused again. "One of the fellows came over to me and told me Matthew had already left on one of the earlier trucks."

Peter gave a mild gasp and looked at Corey, who was sitting still, his eyes going from Lillian to Peter.

"I became empty, cold and alone in Seattle. The constant rain didn't help. Yes, I continued with nursing school, thinking that if I became an RN at least my life would get back to 'normal,' as I'd been before I'd met Matthew, whatever 'normal' was. So after I got registered, I worked a few years at a Seattle hospital to get my experience, then came back to La Sangre. Since then I've been here," she looked at Peter and Corey, "still empty, cold and alone."

There was silence. Corey didn't know what to say, while Peter chose his words carefully. "Lillian," he said softly, "I'm sorry, but that guy was a sleazeball. I've known some guys like that. They just looked better and had a lot of money."

"Oh, I'm sure he was," she sighed. "but you know, I don't think any of us can say 'If I knew then what I know now,' because I knew it, young and silly as I was. I just chose not to look at it.

It's funny, I can forgive Matthew for deserting me, but I still can't forgive myself for what I did." She looked at Peter. "Not until this weekend. Not until now."

Peter nodded, knowing Lillian wasn't making a romantic overture. They were people, middle-aged people, together, understanding. A thought struck Peter. "Why does it take so long," he asked Lillian, "to forgive someone, or to forgive ourselves? Why does it *have* to take so long?"

"I guess," Lillian mused, "I guess we just can't understand the magnitude of God's forgiveness, and we chain ourselves down to our own limited capability. God gives us free choice to do what we want, and to forgive each other, and ourselves. His forgiveness is unlimited, but ours is limited by our own weaknesses, our own fears. Even, and especially, by our own self-loathing."

Sal was still standing at the cliff by the hairpin turn. He couldn't do it. Somewhere he'd heard that "If you have the guts to commit suicide, you have the guts to face and deal with your problems."

On an impulse he walked to Lillian's cottage thinking he'd talk to her, maybe even confess what he'd done, but he stopped outside when he saw her with Peter and Corey, sitting at the table, deep in conversation. They wouldn't be able to see him; it was dark and the moon hadn't yet risen high enough to bathe La Sangre with its light. Besides, anyone who saw the Pastor walking around La Sangre at night, especially on a Saturday night, knew that he was just practicing his sermon for Sunday morning, as well as praying for a covering of protection over the town. It made the townspeople feel secure and comforted to see their Pastor walking around at night, in prayer. But now, it was Sal who needed comfort, and he wished he could join Lillian, Peter and Corey.

But he couldn't. Not anymore. They, everyone, was cut off from him. In desperation Sal walked further south to where the path ended at the Owens' cottage. Unlike all the other houses, especially on the night of the full moon, the shades were still drawn. Against the bedroom shade he could discern flickering candlelight. The last thing Sal wanted was to go back into that hell hole, or if he did go back in there, it would be a fantasy attempt to walk backwards out of that house, to reverse time to where he was before.

And just where were you, before all this, Sal? Where were you early this morning? You were standing proudly at the hairpin turn, smug in your perceived upcoming battle with Satan.

The voice was back in full force, as if Sal's avoiding suicide had made it even stronger, more desperate.

And now where are you, Sal? After calling Corey, your "son," a bastard, after telling Doyle to steal Pete's battery, after telling Mary not to let Pete Freeman make any outbound calls. And after going to Jessie's house with the purpose of telling her not to give Pete Freeman a ride out of town? It was stupid to go back there Sal, just plain stupid. You should have just called her. You knew this afternoon when you talked to Jessie that you should stay away from her. You were warned. She was leaving tomorrow and you should have just stayed away and let it be. But no, you went anyway.

And then you committed adultery. The Pastor Salvatore Satori had committed adultery with one of his parishioners. ("Sal," Jessie had told him, "it took me a lifetime to understand something, and you need to know this: we're not sinners because we sin. We *sin* because we're *sinners*.")

It wasn't true. It couldn't be true. He couldn't allow that, couldn't make excuses for what he did, to say it's okay because I'm a sinner. ("Just remember that and stop *thinking* so damned much, and you'll be fine.") Nothing made sense anymore. This morning he was certain God had told him that Satan was on his way to La Sangre. He had sensed trouble, there was no doubt. Was he making up voices?

Face it Sal. You're just plain crazy. You always have been, creating and believing your own agenda. And as such you've failed. Failed as a husband, as a father, and yes, as a pastor.

Sal gasped at the sucker-punch. He must have been holding his breath for two minutes.

Okay, he was crazy, *is* crazy. At least that was something he could work with.

But no, even that didn't feel right, much as he would allow the possibility. He took another deep breath and exhaled. Breathe in, breathe out.

The only thing he did know for sure was that he was tired, 38 years tired. He couldn't think any more. He needed to rest. He walked north towards his home. As he passed the various houses, their doors unlocked, the window shades up in anticipation of the moon shining into their modest homes, he knew it would be the last walk through town for Pastor Salvatore Satori.

He stopped outside his home. Besides rest, he needed a shower. Better yet, a swim in the ocean, so the salt water could purify him, expunge his stink, a stink that had seemed so wonderfully nasty when he lay on Jessie's kitchen floor. Now, it was just foul. But there wasn't a path to the ocean from or around La Sangre, the only way to it was to jump, and that was no longer an option. So he had to shower at his house, he'd have to face Connie...and himself.

Sal saw Connie through the window, on the phone, looking worried. She should be, he never missed dinner. Normally it wasn't until after dinner that he would go out and walk around the town, praying and protecting his flock. He continued to watch Connie on the phone, though he couldn't hear her.

"Lillian? It's Connie. Have you seen Sal?"

"No." Lillian ransacked for the last time she had seen him, and then winced in memory of her scene with him in the Satori kitchen, when she screamed like a fishwife. "No, not since this afternoon at your place. Why?"

"He hasn't come home for dinner. I've looked around the bluff, as far as I can see from the deck anyway, and he doesn't seem to be anywhere."

"Connie," Lillian lowered her voice. Her phone was in her bedroom, out of earshot of Peter and Corey. "I'm sure Sal's all right. Listen, why don't you come over? Just to say hello."

"I couldn't."

Lillian knew that Mary could be listening in, and probably was, but she didn't care anymore. "You don't have to tell Peter who you are. You said he didn't recognize you today. Just come over so you can see."

"No Lillian. I can't. There's something wrong with Sal, and it might make it worse if I were to...I just can't see Peter with Corey."

"Are you sure? Maybe if you do, it might re-solve something. You've been carrying this for a long time."

"How do they look," Connie faltered, "to-gether I mean?"

"They're beautiful Connie."

Connie wanted to see them, she really did. But given the precarious state she and Sal were now in, it might push everything over the edge. Just like...

Just like falling off a cliff.

"Connie?" Lillian asked.

Connie let the receiver drop out of her hand and ran out of the house, into the light of the full moon.

Sal went inside after Connie ran out of the house. He showered and changed within ten minutes, grateful neither she nor Corey re-turned. He still felt filthy after the shower, filthy and tired. But the smell was gone, and he felt presentable enough to go into the church.

Presentable. Right. Somehow that must be all he'd been doing his 12 years in La Sangre, be-ing "presentable."

But he was also tired, very tired, and he couldn't think any more. ("You *think* too much, Sal!")

He walked up to the church that stood by

itself, facing Route 1, its sign announcing to drivers that it was the La Sangre Christian Church. It was clean and white, simple and inviting.

Inviting to *you*, Sal? Shower or no shower, you're still an adulterer.

He ignored the voice and proceeded to the church, not for any promise of sanctuary, although maybe that voice couldn't get through the church doors. But whether or not it could, Sal just needed a place to lay down for a while.

He opened the unlocked door of the church and went inside. Mercifully, it was empty. The full moon was streaming through the stained-glass windows, creating a strange and beautiful color mixture on the pews and wooden floor. He walked down the aisle and sat on the right front pew. After a minute, he stretched out on the hard wooden pew and fell asleep within seconds.

Jay walked into the church as soon as Sal was asleep. He proceeded down the aisle and stood over Sal, studying him for a moment. Then he sat down on the pew and lifted Sal's head, gently so he wouldn't wake him, and placed it on his lap. He placed his right hand on Sal's chest. Then Jay began to pray.

SIXTEEN

Lillian waited for a dial tone to know if Connie had hung up, but there was none. She tapped the button several times, and Mary came on. The loud click told Lillian that Mary hadn't been on the line.

"Good evening, this is Mary. Praise the Lord!"

"Hi Mary, it's Nurse Walker. I was just talking to Connie...to Sister Satori on the phone. Were we disconnected?"

"Just a moment, Nurse Walker, and I'll check. No, her line is active. Is anything wrong?"

"I don't know. I just wondered if she had hung up or not. I know there's been a problem with the phones today."

"A problem? I didn't know that anyone has had a problem today."

"I thought that no one in town could dial out."

"No, the phones are fine, both incoming and outgoing. Why, have you been having trouble?"

Lillian's gasp escaped her before she could

stop it, and the gasp slapped Mary into remembering the lie she'd told Lillian, Corey, and the football player that afternoon. Even over the phone line, unable to see each other, Lillian knew that Mary knew that she was caught. Mary's retraction was ridiculous.

"Oh that's right Nurse Walker," she said too hurriedly. "I'd forgotten, how silly of me. Yes, there *are* no calls going out. I don't know why I didn't think..."

Lillian hung up the phone, deciding that mindless Christians make lousy liars. But why was Mary lying? Who had instructed her to do so?

The Pastor of course. The same person who wouldn't let anyone in La Sangre have their own phone lines, who had his own private line that even his own wife and son couldn't use. The Owens were the only other family that had their own line, even the Pastor couldn't prevent them from doing that. He's not god of the phone company.

But why was he keeping Peter captive here? Was Peter in some kind of trouble? Does Sal know that Peter is Corey's father—and Connie doesn't know he knows—and now he's seeking some kind of sick revenge?

This whole town is sick, Lillian proclaimed, and its sickness (and wellness, she self-admitted) was increasing exponentially this weekend.

She wondered if Peter, just by his presence, his arrival today in town, was a catalyst that put him in some kind of danger from Sal. ("He's going to tear this town apart!" Connie had cried.)

Lillian went into the dining room, where Peter and Corey were talking football again, and waited for a break in the conversation. "Corey, I was just talking with your mother, and we got disconnected. I can't get her back on the phone, and I'm a little concerned. Would you mind running over and checking on her for me?"

Corey read Lillian's concern and stood up to leave.

"I'll go with you," Peter said.

"Uh...no Peter," Lillian ransacked for a reason. "Listen, I'm going over to the Owens' cottage for something. How about you go on down to the cliff, look at the ocean in the moonlight. It's a full moon tonight. I'll join you there in a few minutes, okay?"

Peter and Corey looked at each other, both shrugged, and Corey left.

From the door Lillian pointed for Peter to see, "Just follow that path there. It leads you straight to the cliff. Be careful."

Jessie couldn't sleep. She lay in her bed, watching the flickering candle. What *was* it that was bothering her? Oh yes, it was something she still had to do. But *what*? She was leaving tomorrow morning, before church even. She'd thought about proceeding as usual with her La Sangre charade: going to church, and this time she could quietly gloat over the hypocritical Pastor Salvatore Satori preaching to his congregation about the wages of sin. She could even go to the Father's Day picnic afterward, bustling around with the other ladies at the picnic tables behind the church, making sure the potato salad and condiments for the grilled chicken, hamburgers and hot dogs were set out. How she would love to watch Pastor Satori walk around, shaking hands, and wishing everyone a Happy Father's Day.

But no, she couldn't indulge herself in that, she had to stay alert. Gloating can dull your responses, make you lazy and overconfident, especially when there's something more to do.

Something more to do, yes, but what?

There was a knock on the door. Maybe that will answer her question. She got out of bed, put on her robe, went to the door and unlocked it. After nine months of living here, does anyone know she locks her door?

It was Lillian, 'Nurse Walker,' standing on the porch.

"Hi Jessie, did I wake you up?"

"I wasn't asleep," Jessie sighed lightly. "What's going on?"

"Well, there's apparently a problem with

the La Sangre phone lines. I know the Owens have their own line, can I use your phone? It's important."

Jessie shook her head. "It's been shut off. I had it shut off this morning. The Owens wanted me to change the billing when I left so they wouldn't be stuck with my long distance phone calls. They'll restart the service in their name when they get here. The same with the electricity, it gets shut off tomorrow. I guess they don't trust me not to skip out on my bills."

I don't trust you either, Lillian realized. Not after this morning, after your flippant regard of Corey's damaged graduation cake. "When will the Owens be back?"

"Monday, they said."

"Oh." Lillian thought quickly. "Jessie, what time are you leaving tomorrow?"

"Early. I don't think I'm going to church."

"Well, do you think you could give Pete Freeman a ride out of town?"

"Who's that?"

"The football player. He was in the Saloon earlier today."

"Oh, the guy that fainted. What's *his* problem?"

"He needs a new battery for his truck. He can call Triple-A when he gets to Santa Rosa and ride back with them."

"Well Lillian, I'm not going through Santa

Rosa, I'm taking Highway 1 back down the coast to San Francisco. Besides, I'll have the passenger seat loaded up with my clothes, other personal stuff. It's a sports car, after all."

She may as well have given me a firm "no," Lillian knew. There was no point in pursuing it. She turned to leave, not bothering with a "Goodbye." There was nothing "good" about Jessie Malana.

"Say," Jessie asked the retreating Lillian, "what's with this football guy anyway? Who is he? *What* is he?"

Lillian just kept walking.

And is that football guy part of my unfinished business? Jessie wondered.

Connie stood at the cliff. It was one of the most beautiful full moon nights she'd seen in La Sangre, just enough clouds to scatter and play with the moonlight, adding more depth and mystery to the sky and sea than usual. Perfect for hearing God. She *had* to hear Him tonight.

"Father in heaven," she prayed out loud, "let me and Sal see the Truth, Your Truth..."

She stopped. Connie had experienced those times, however few, that we hear God's voice loudly and clearly, if not exactly audibly.

I heard you the first time Connie, He said, when you prayed earlier. His Word was simple and concise, and not without a trace of humor.

Connie smiled. Thank you, she said silently.
"Hello!"

She didn't jump like she had with Lillian. She knew that voice. "Hello Peter," she said even as she was still turning to him.

"Oh," he smiled. "I guess Corey told you about me."

She nodded to him. "I saw you in the Saloon this afternoon." His voice, his smile. And she could still feel his touch from all those years ago.

"Oh yeah, Corey's a big fan. I guess your husband is too. I thought they recognized me in the Saloon."

"So did I."

"Corey and I just had dinner with Lillian. That's a good boy you've got."

"You too."

What? Peter half-smiled uncertainly. I guess she must mean that I'm a good boy too. Okay.

Connie smiled at him. Peter was always so easy to read, so open, so...*there*. He didn't know what I meant, and it might not be the right time, not yet anyway.

"By the way," Peter said, "when we were at Lillian's house, she thought something was wrong, because she got disconnected from you. So she sent Corey to your house to check. Did he find you?"

"No. I came out here. But I'm all right. Yes, I did let the receiver drop. I'll call her back."

"She's not there right now. She said she was going to the...Owens cottage, I think. So I came out here." Peter turned to the ocean. "Beautiful." In all his 34 years in California, he'd never seen the Pacific Ocean this way.

"Yes," Connie looked at Peter, "beautiful." The moonlight highlighted his blonde hair, his bright blue eyes. Had there been a full moon that night in Bakersfield? She thought so. She remembered how he had looked that night, glowing, as he did now. Yes, it was time.

"Peter, you probably don't remember me, but we knew each other in Bakersfield. "I'm...or I *was,* Connie O'Hara."

Peter's eyes sharpened in instant recognition. "Connie..." He looked into her eyes, seeing her and knowing her (*really* seeing and knowing her like before, Connie noticed). He looked down at her full figure, not at all heavy, the perfect hourglass, and then back into her eyes. "I'm sorry...I didn't recognize you." He shook his head as if in a dream. "I...haven't seen you since..."

"Since high school, I know. I've changed, haven't I? No more Connie-Cooty."

"You never were."

"Not to you I wasn't."

Their study of each other was like a caress, warm and comfortable, remembering.

Peter spoke first. "Connie, you didn't go to

our ten year reunion. I looked for you there, even asked about you, but the committee said they couldn't find you."

Connie shrugged. "My parents are still there, in the same house. The committee could have found me if they wanted to. But I didn't want to go anyway. My husband, Sal, wanted to. He's a big Forty-Niners fan, and he knows you're from Bakersfield High, so he thought you might be there. But I told him I didn't want to go."

They continued to study each other as Peter held out his hands. Nothing had changed. They hadn't changed.

"I used to wonder if you remembered me," Connie told him, taking his hands and not taking her eyes off his. "I was sure you didn't, especially after you became so famous. I watched you play football. Sal and Corey and I hardly ever missed a game, except on Sunday evenings. We went to the Monday night home games at Candlestick whenever we could. You were great."

"Thanks, but Connie I *never* forgot you. I tried to see you again after...after graduation. I went to your house, but your parents said that you'd gone to live with an aunt. They were kind of cold to me. They wouldn't tell me anything, wouldn't even give me your address so I could write to you."

He had come by to see her! He wanted to write to her! Her parents never told her. Why didn't they?

"I...yes, I was living with an aunt in Fresno," Connie said, restraining tears.

"I went by again, just before I went to college, thinking maybe you were back home, and they said you were getting married. That was all they'd tell me."

"Yes...I met Sal in Fresno, and...well everything moved so quickly." Connie shook her head, wondering how things had worked out, seemingly against her. It wasn't fair. "I guess I just...went ahead with things, with what I felt I was supposed to do. We got married, and we had Corey early the next year." She wondered if Peter would do the math, but it didn't matter, there was still time to tell him. "We moved up here when Sal got the job five years later. We've been here twelve years. I'm a Pastor's wife. Everything just...happened. I didn't really question it. I don't think I ever have, not until today."

"Connie," Peter said after a moment, "I know you're married, and I respect that, but I have to know. That night, it seemed so *real*, just the opposite of high school, which now seems like it was some kind of TV game show, where you play by the rules to win the prize. It was that same way at the ten year reunion, you sure didn't miss anything. It was all about who made the most money, who had the biggest house, the best-looking spouse, and who hadn't gotten fat and bald."

That Connie had also thought of the game show metaphor earlier that day wasn't lost on her. Were they still that close? "Well, you must have been the winner at the Bakersfield High School Reunion, Pete Freeman, Superbowl Champ."

Peter shook his head. "That was before the Superbowl; but either way they didn't care about me, just the celebrity, asking me what Joe Montana's like, all of that. And it was scary because *everyone* felt that way. I never felt so alone in my life, and after that, it was like everything flip-flopped, and maybe that night with you wasn't real after all, but everything *else* was real, and I couldn't get with it. Connie, do you know what I mean?"

"Yes Peter," she nodded. "Yes I do."

"I have to know Connie, was that night real? For you?"

Connie gave up on fighting the tears. "It was real," she sobbed. "And everything else," she turned and looked at La Sangre, "has been a TV game show, like you say. I've known it all these years, but I never wanted to admit it."

"Then...did we blow it?"

Connie turned from La Sangre back to Peter. He had tears in his eyes. "I don't know Peter. Somehow I don't think so. It's hard to figure out what the right thing is. And I'm worried that our...that my son might make the wrong choices.

I want him to do the right thing for himself."

"I feel the same way about him," Peter nodded. "He's a good kid. He reminds me of myself at that age."

Connie nearly choked on her tears. "Yes... very much so." How long can she go on like this? "And... he's very drawn to you."

"I don't know why. I hope it's not just because of football."

"No," Connie shook her head, looking out to the ocean. "It's more than just that." Tell him Connie!

"What do you mean?"

Connie ignored the question. "Do you mind... do you have a handkerchief?"

He reached into his right hip pocket and gave her his, thinking it best not to wipe her tears for her.

"Thank you." She blotted her eyes. "May I keep this?"

"Please do." He waited a moment. "So tell me, what about Corey's father? Is he a good father to him?"

Connie smiled to herself at the ironic question and turned back to the ocean. "Sal loves Corey, but I don't think he knows how to just let Corey be. He's trying to control him."

"Like my father did to me," Peter nodded, thoroughly and finally understanding. ("What I wanted," he'd told Jay, "was to somehow recreate myself, make a perfect and unblemished me, that I could love and accept.")

"Peter," Connie turned back to him, "thank you, for loving me like you did. Thank you."

"It was easy," he said. "But up until now, I've been wondering if I had or not, loved you. Or loved anyone."

"You did. You loved me. You called me Connie, not Connie-Cooty. You sat next to me in the school bus when the others wouldn't, you defended me, you talked to me, you listened to me, you danced with me..."

"'When A Man Loves A Woman.'" Peter's voice broke.

"...and you made love to me in the fields of Bakersfield. If that isn't love, then nothing else is."

Peter's tears flowed, unafraid. For once in his life, if only that once, he had loved, he had really loved.

"Would you do me favor?" Connie asked.

Peter nodded.

"Would you give me a hug? Just for old times' sake? For Connie-Cooty?"

"Not for Connie-Cooty," he shook his head, "for Connie O'Hara." He put his arms around her.

"Peter Freeman," she whispered, her head against his strong shoulder. It felt the same after all these years. She'd never forgotten how it felt.

The knocking on Jessie's front door was incessant. It couldn't be Lillian again. She'd left for good, it was obvious by her abrupt departure. Besides, this knock was stronger, steadier, masculine.

"NO!" Jessie screamed from her bedroom. In the dark, with the candlelight, she was back in her father's home, with the incessant knocking on her bedroom door.

"NO!"

"Please Jessie, let me in." But this time it wasn't her father. She knew who it was, knocking on the cottage door. His voice was strong but kind, soft and encouraging. "Jessie, please!"

Yes, she knew who he was. He'd come into the Saloon this morning with that football player.

"GET AWAY FROM ME! GOD DAMN YOU! LEAVE ME ALONE!"

SEVENTEEN

Lillian had planned to go from Jessie's cottage over to the cliff where she would join Peter, but she went home instead. Something wasn't right, and it was triggered by her meeting with Jessie. Yes, Jessie was now showing her true colors, but Lillian had seen that all along, hadn't she? That was why she had tried to align herself with Jessie. It should have been easy to align with her, working across the road from each other and at the church and the women's groups. But Lillian's attempts were to no avail... which was fine, she'd finally decided. But why had it been so important to her?

Because I hated men, Lillian admitted as she walked to her home. And I knew Jessie hated men too. For me, it had started with Matthew and not until this evening had I truly forgiven Matthew for deserting me, for making me destroy my only child, with whom I wouldn't be so alone today. I would have raised my child on my own, my nurse's salary providing for us. I'd have a family today, probably be a grandmother by now. But no, I gave that up for Matthew.

Matthew. He had shown me how to feel, how to love, how to be a woman, and then had left me, cold and alone. I've hated Matthew all these years, swearing vengeance, and in turn I've hated all men for what they do to women. They use us, victimize us, and then desert us. All men are like that, and that's why I returned to La Sangre and took up a nun's existence. I wasn't going to let another man exercise his power over me. I would take care of myself.

Then, right after my return, Sal Satori came to La Sangre and started to take over the town, buying up the businesses and exerting a unifying control that some people welcomed and so remained, and others hated, eventually selling their homes and leaving. Sal had obtained a real estate license and offered the sellers a low percentage fee for him to represent them, allowing him to search for potential buyers at his discretion through churches in the Santa Rosa area. Moreover, he screened them for their naivety and gullibility, feeding his fast-growing narcissism. Only the Owens weren't swayed. They held onto their home and staunchly avoided the snares of Pastor Satori and La Sangre.

Lillian loved God, she always had, but she had begun to hate self-professed Christians. She hated their judgment, pretense, patronizing, charade, and what she saw was rapidly becoming a cult in La Sangre, where people couldn't think for themselves. So she had decided to stay and fight in her own quiet "Nurse Walker" way. She awaited the day when she could bring Salvatore Satori, and everything he represented, down to his knees.

And that day had come. She had known this morning that a monster would be let loose in the town, and at first she had been afraid, afraid that the monster was evil, that it would feed and encourage the fear and mistrust that everyone in La Sangre disguised as calm and cool Christian virtue. But now she knew her fear was from the fact that she herself would have to face the monster, the monster of herself. The monster in her that had so wantonly attacked Sal in his own home this morning, nearly castrating the man. It was revenge, pure and simple. Revenge against Matthew through Sal.

Lillian found herself standing in the living room of her small home, a home that just minutes ago was so full of love, with Peter and Corey, two men no less, a man and his son. But now it was so lonely, worse than it had ever been.

"I'm sorry." It was all she could say. "Please help me, forgive me."

Suddenly it was over and in came the calm. That wonderful calm that despite her quiet, mature demeanor, she hadn't felt in years... if indeed she'd ever felt it, particularly during her youthful quest for "excitement." Her past, her anger, her hate, all of it was gone. Even her pride, which up until now she was unaware of. ("Everyone likes me," she'd smugly told Peter and Corey.) Yes, that was true, everyone liked her, but Lillian had unknowingly worn it as a badge, as pride of ownership.

Cut yourself some slack Lillian. Remember that you also said to Peter and Corey, "It's a blessing." Yes, blessings come from God, they're not our own doing.

Okay, she agreed. But I do owe Sal an apology. I had no right to talk to him like that. It was between him and Connie. I had no business standing up and fighting for her, she'll have to do that herself.

Lillian sat down on the couch, enjoying this new calm, hearing the ocean outside her window, as if its loving roar had been suspended during her brutal self-realization. She closed her eyes. Yes, it was all over.

Except something else was going to happen, still, and she knew it. It had been confirmed during her brief visit with Jessie. Father's Day would be here in a few hours. What was going to happen? What was she going to have to do?

That's an easy one, Lillian. Just clear the dining room table, let the dishes soak, and go to bed. We'll discuss it tomorrow. You've done enough for one day.

"Hey!" Corey greeted Peter and Connie good-naturedly. "What are you doing with your arm around my Mom?"

Peter turned to him and held out his other arm. "Don't you know that your mother and I are old friends from Bakersfield?"

Corey looked at his mother. "Mom?"

"I was going to tell you Corey," she said, "I just haven't had the chance yet."

"But why didn't you mention it before this?" Corey said, excited. "Tell me!"

"In a bit Corey," Peter said. "For now let's just look at the ocean, the moon on the water." Corey stepped in and Peter had his arms around the two of them.

The three of them were quiet. Everything now made sense to Connie; she had a sense of completion. Corey was just happy with Pete Freeman's arm around him. And Peter knew he had come full circle. His arm around Corey was like sitting on his father's shoulders in the dream ("This is all yours, Pete."). All his. Suddenly, at last, he loved and missed his father. But...did his father love him?

Yes, he did, Peter knew, undoubtedly and finally. He loved me. He did the best he could with what he had. He threw the football with me in the back yard. ("Nice arm, kid!") He built up a big company, supported us well, lots of toys at Christmas, nice vacations to Hawaii and Florida.

We had things we never would have had, not like most of my friends in Bakersfield. Even if I hadn't gotten the sports scholarship, Dad would have been able to pay for my college education. Peter closed his eyes to himself. I never thanked him for that. I thought there was all the time in the world for that stuff.

Thank you, Peter said silently to his father. And thank you God.

You're very welcome Peter.

Doyle jolted awake. It was that dream again. No, that nightmare. He'd had it since he was a child, but now it was coming more often. Two nights in a row now, last night and tonight. He hadn't meant to fall asleep. He was sitting on his bed waiting for Corey to arrive and go into his room. It would be Corey's first night here, and Doyle had promised the Pastor that he would watch over him. But somehow Doyle had fallen asleep and had that nightmare.

It was still disjointed, but the images were no longer painful flashes, they were extending themselves, creating a frightening flow. Walking down the dirt road from their house in McCarthy, Texas. Doyle loved to walk, loved the clouds, loved the sun. Desolate as West Texas could be, its infinite reach held promises for him. He was a happy boy.

Then the old shack, owned by old man...what

was his name? The kids called him the Crazy Man In The Haunted Shack, like one of those cheap horror movies they'd watch at the Golden Theater in McCarthy.

So Doyle was walking down the dirt road past the shack, a dirty gray shack with a red door. The old man came out and beckoned him. Come on inside Doyle! I have something for you. A present!

With the trusting innocence of a child, Doyle went inside.

Another bright flash in the nightmare, and Sheriff Turner is asking Doyle questions. His mother is crying, and he'd never seen his father so angry. ("If it was my daughter, I'd kill him myself!" his father was shouting at Sheriff Turner.)

Another flash.

It hurts to go to the bathroom, Doyle cries to his mother.

I know honey, she said soothingly. The doctor said it will hurt for a while, but it'll get better. We have to put the ointment there, and take the pills the doctor gave us, okay Doyle?

But it hurts me when you put that stuff inside me.

I know it does, sweetheart, but it'll make you better. We only have to do it for a while.

Flash.

He doesn't remember a thing, Doyle

overhears his mother telling his father. It's a blessing from God.

I'll kill the son-of-a-bitch, his father says.

He's gone now, Wayne, his mother insists, put away for good. The Sheriff said he'll never be back. Doyle doesn't remember anything and hopefully he never will. We have to move on, put it behind us. God wants us to forgive.

I'll never forgive that son-of-a-bitch.

That nightmare, coming back to Doyle like that, sharper and more in focus, it has to be an attack by Satan. Doyle knew it was. He saw Satan this morning, with that football player. Satan, wearing the red shirt, the devil's color. And that dog, the red dog. The Devil Dog, the Hound of Hell. And now Doyle was being attacked with Satanic dreams. God wouldn't make him have dreams like that. God made us forget, made everything feel good, like those pills his mother had him take for a year, maybe two years after... after...

After *what* Doyle?

No! It hurts! It's not of God! God loved us so much that He enabled us not to have to think or worry. He made us not have to question anything, made us not have to make decisions or deal with anything that might hurt us. God made us *happy*.

Doyle sat up on the bed. But there's something else that wasn't a dream. Doyle knew he couldn't ascribe it to God or to Satan. It was something that had really happened.

He was fifteen, in high school, the small high school that McCarthy, Texas shared with two small neighboring towns. There was a girl he liked. She lived in one of the other towns, took the same bus to school that he did. One Saturday Doyle walked five miles to see her. It had taken him over a year to work up the nerve to visit her, and twice while walking he had almost turned around on the dirt road from McCarthy. The first time he almost turned back was when he saw the rotted shack. It was barely standing; windows broken out and paint peeling, but the door still unmistakably red. He didn't know why it still scared him, it wasn't haunted like they used to call it. Still, he walked on the opposite side of the road from it.

The girl had smiled when she answered the door, said she was glad to see him, and invited him in. He talked with her in the kitchen, drinking lemonade, while her parents watched the news on TV in the living room. President Eisenhower was speaking. Doyle told the girl that after he graduated from high school he was going to El Paso to auto mechanic school. He was already taking automotive classes in high school, and the teacher said he was good. (It was nice, Doyle thought, to be told I was "good.")

The girl was listening to him, barely

interested, and she kept turning around to her parents in the living room, bothered by them. She even seemed as if she hated them. Why? He didn't hate his own parents, why should she hate hers? But she was very pretty, and she was nice to Doyle.

Then her parents shut off the TV and announced they were going visiting, and they would be back later. Doyle got up to leave, but they said he could stay, maybe watch TV, he seemed like such a nice young man; tall and skinny, her mother smiled at him, but nice looking. "Oh, that's all right boy," her father had given his skinny bicep a friendly squeeze, "you'll fill out!" (Doyle liked that. The auto mechanic teacher had told him he was "good," and now the girl's mother said he was "nice looking," and the father had encouraged his growth and even squeezed his arm.) They'll see him when they come back, they promised. They won't be gone long. And then they left.

And then, Doyle remembered, as he sat on his bed in his little room above the La Sangre Last Chance Gas Station and Garage, and then that whore, that little slut, said hurry up, let's go into my bedroom, we have time before they get back. Surprised, shocked even, Doyle thought he knew what she meant, but he wasn't positive, and so he followed her into her bedroom. She took her clothes off (like old man what's-his-name, in the nightmares he was now having), and she was naked. It scared Doyle, and he was afraid to look. She told Doyle to take his clothes off too (like the old man in the nightmare had said). But he was scared and just stood there, so she came over to him and unbuckled his belt and pulled his pants down because she said he was taking too long.

Hurry up! she had ordered. We don't have much time! What's wrong? Are you scared? Hurry!

She was getting mad, and Doyle got more scared, and she got madder because he was getting more scared.

What's the matter with you Doyle? she screamed at him, angry. Why can't you do it? Is it because you like *boys* instead of *girls*?

And then Doyle had pulled up his pants and run out of the house, down the road, back to his home in McCarthy. ("Do you like *boys* instead of *girls*?" she had screamed at him as he ran away.) And Doyle kept running, trying to get away from his own body, trying to run outside of his own skin. He hated himself, he hated his body, he hated sex, he hated that girl. That...whore. That was it: she was a whore. Not pure, not saintly, not holy, but a dirty whore who will burn in hell.

Sitting on his bed, breathing hard, Doyle looked around him, at his room, at the window that faced the road and the ocean. It's all right. He was here now, in La Sangre. He'd found his way here from Texas. He'd never gone to auto mechanic school, but used his natural skill to keep moving west, working at different gas stations as a lay mechanic and tow truck driver. Eventually he landed in Santa Rosa, saw a Help Wanted ad in the paper, and somehow got a ride to La Sangre.

Doyle met the Pastor and he knew he was home. He loved the Pastor, loved his saintly wife, and loved La Sangre. A nice small salary and a room over the garage. His meals in the Saloon were covered. He could even have a steak if he wanted.

Doyle took a deep breath and closed his eyes. God had delivered him to La Sangre. This was his home, and he was protected. He'll never have to wander any more. He'll just pray for those nightmares to end, and God will see to it.

"Sal?" Connie found him in the church, lying on the right front pew.

Sal opened his eyes and saw Connie, his wife, standing over him.

"Are you all right?" she asked him. She thought it strange that this was the last place she'd thought to look, but then usually he was outside, especially on such a nice evening.

He sat up slowly. "Yeah, I'm all right," he nodded automatically. Then he considered his response. "Yes, I am," he looked at her, "I *am* all right."

"I've been worried."

"I know, I'm sorry. I should have told you I'd be late for dinner."

"I went to the cliff; I didn't see you."

"The cliff," Sal repeated quietly. His consideration of suicide was as idiotic as the adultery. Neither of them were Sal. Whoever "Sal" is.

The moonlight streaming through the stained glass windows cast an ethereal light on Sal's dark eyes. He's looking at me, Connie saw, really looking at me. And he's going to listen to me. Is this a fluke, or is it the start of something new? In case it was the former, Connie made a fast prayer for the right words. It was like having only one wish from the genie, you want to make sure it's the right one. She sat down on the pew, a few feet from Sal.

"Oh Sal, I've just discovered what a fool I've been."

"That makes two of us."

"All these years, these twelve years in La Sangre especially, I've been *performing*, playing a part, like some bizarre combination of Tammy Faye Bakker and...I don't know, Carol Brady."

"So what does that make me, Jim Bakker and Mike Brady?"

He's listening to me, and how about this new sense of humor between them. "Hardly," she answered.

"You neither." He held his arm out to her. "Well Connie O'Hara, I'd like you to meet Salvatore Anthony Satori."

She scooted over and enveloped herself in his arm. "And just who is that, pray tell?"

"I don't know, but I'm going to find out. With your help. And God's."

Connie rested her head on his shoulder. What large, strong shoulders he has! Did she ever realize that, or appreciate it? Is it possible to be married to someone for 17 years and not know what strong shoulders he has? His arm around her felt different too. Powerful and secure. Had it always been that way? Of course they'd had sex, rather functional and dutiful sex. But had they ever really touched each other? She'd never questioned it. Where had she been?

You know where you've been Connie-Cooty. You know where you've been all these years. You were back in high school. Well, it's time to grow up.

Yes it is, Connie O'Hara Satori, she told herself. It's time to grow up.

Doyle was still sitting on his bed. He hadn't moved since the Satanic dream and the memory of that little whore. The memory may be real, something horrible from his youth that, if he prays enough, God will erase. But the dream was definitely from Satan.

GARY KYRIAZI

As if in confirmation, there was a knock on the door, a steady, insistent knock. Not too loud, but firm and solid.

Was that Satan at his door?

"Let me in Doyle," a voice said.

Something told Doyle that the voice couldn't be Satan, it was too nice.

But Doyle, you know that Satan can have a very pleasing presence.

Yes, it *has* to be Satan! Who else could it be, to frighten him like this? It was Satan who was giving him those nightmares and making him remember that Texas whore so vividly.

"Doyle?" the voice said.

"Get behind me Satan!" Doyle cried.

"Doyle, let me in." His voice was firm and encouraging, but Doyle knew such a voice could sound attractive, like a wolf in sheep's clothing, just like the Bible warns us of. "Doyle, please!"

Summoning all his courage, Doyle screamed out loud, "GOD, GIVE ME THE STRENGTH TO DEFEAT SATAN!" He rushed to the door and flung it open.

Corey and the football player were stopped on the landing, staring at him. Corey had some towels and a small suitcase, the football player had a small overnight bag.

"Was that you knocking on my door?" Doyle, still in screaming mode, asked Corey.

"Not us," Corey glanced at Peter.

Then Doyle looked down at the stairs. That's what he heard. It must have been the sound of these two coming up the stairs. Not Satan knocking on the door.

Maybe it was *someone else* knocking on the door, Doyle. Not Satan. Someone else.

No Doyle. You asked God to give you the strength to defeat Satan, and when you flung open the door, who was there? The football player, right? Get it?

"Pete is staying here tonight," Corey said, frowning at Doyle's more-than-usual odd behavior.

"Oh," Doyle said. He turned his look from the stairs to Peter.

"What were you screaming about anyway?" Corey asked.

Doyle leaned against the door jamb, his eyes still on Peter. "I was praying. Praying for strength."

Peter looked at Corey.

"It sure didn't sound like it." Corey returned Peter's glance and then shrugged. "Well..."

Corey opened the door to his room and Peter followed, closing the door behind him.

Doyle continued to lean against the door jamb, looking at Corey's closed door, remembering his promise to the Pastor that he'd keep an eye on Corey.

And with that football player—Satan, or at least Satan's disciple—here, he sure will.

"Hey Pete," Corey said when they were settled in bed.

"Yeah?"

"You said something today about going up to Eureka."

Eureka. Jay had said he was going there. But now Peter didn't need to go to Eureka. Where he was didn't matter anymore. "Yeah, I thought about it, but now I don't know."

"What are you going to do?"

"I don't know." Was he going to stay in La Sangre, because of Connie? He didn't think so. Out at the cliff he'd received a clear resolution that he and Connie were of the past, with a shared appreciation of their history together. They had both come full circle, individually and together, but there was no future for them as a couple. They both knew that. It was like Kristi and him talking earlier today at O'Mahony's. A shared appreciation, and then time to move on.

Move on to what?

"I don't know," Peter repeated to Corey. "Maybe I'll just drive up north for a while," he said, "up into Oregon. It's summer, the weather's getting nicer. I'm getting a little tired of the fog in San Francisco. My Mom and two of my sisters are getting a house in Lake Tahoe, I may join them for a while."

Corey summoned all his youthful courage. "Hey Pete?"

"Yeah?"

"Do you think...well, could I come with you, for a while anyway?"

Peter considered it. It wasn't a bad idea. "Well, we'd have to ask your parents, your Dad." He knew Connie would approve and trust him with her son.

"I'm a high school graduate, they have to let me. I don't have much money on me though, just a few bucks Dad gives me for taking care of the church. In fact I have to get up early tomorrow to prepare for the service."

"Oh, don't worry about money. But you're seventeen, we have to ask your parents. If they say okay, we'll have to get some camping equipment, a tent, sleeping bags..."

"I have that stuff."

"All right. We'll ask your parents tomorrow."

"Okay, tomorrow. After church."

"Okay. Good night kid."

"Good night Pete." Corey turned on his side toward the wall. "Pete Freeman," he whispered softly to himself.

Peter heard it, smiled, and turned on his side towards his wall. After wondering how he was going to sleep after his long nap today, he fell into the deepest sleep he'd ever had, as if it was his last. He had a soft and beautiful dream of walking through the orchards in Bakersfield, his father on his left, Corey on his right.

Doyle jolted awake, sweating. The nightmare again. First two nights in a row, now twice in the same night. The scenes extended further, brighter, more focused, merging together into one horrible story.

God help me! Doyle cried. Help me!

You'd better check on Corey, a voice said.

Was that God talking to him? Or Satan? No, the Pastor had told me to keep an eye on Corey, so it must be God. That's probably why He woke me up from Satan's dream. God woke me up to check on Corey.

Grateful that a semblance of order and responsibility would overshadow the Devil Dream, Doyle got up, still fully dressed, shoes still on, and opened his door. The windowless landing was dimly lit by a 60 watt bulb. He stood outside Corey's room, listening. The deep snoring he heard, was that Corey? No, it was the snoring of someone older, a grown man.

It's the football player, remember Doyle? He's in there with Corey.

Yes, Doyle remembered.

Look after Corey, like the Pastor told you to do.

Carefully and quietly Doyle turned the doorknob. It was unlocked. Slowly, very slowly, he opened the door.

Moonlight streamed through the open window of the small room. Corey and the football player were each in their beds, lying on their backs. Corey had a smile on his face. No nightmares for him, Doyle thought with envy. Of course, he's just a kid. Just wait, kid, you'll get yours. He looked over at the football player, also with a peaceful smile on his face, his left wrist draped over his forehead.

Watch out for Corey, the voice said again, like the Pastor told you to do.

Both Corey and the football player were shirtless. Suddenly, in his mind's eye, Doyle saw Corey's young, smooth chest pressed against the football player's well-muscled, blonde-haired chest.

Doyle stifled a gasp. God was telling him something.

He managed to shut the door as quietly as he opened it and stood in the hall, waiting for a message. It came quickly.

The football player was a homosexual! Yes, the football player was a homosexual, and he has seduced Corey!

Damn the homosexuals! Damn them all to hell! They're an abomination to God! They like *boys* instead of *girls*!

Don't go back into that room Doyle. It's evil. Filthy. Sinful. Go tell the Pastor. Tell him that the football player is a homosexual, and he has seduced Corey.

Doyle ran down the stairs, forgetting how

much noise the old wooden stairs made. He had to get to the Pastor.

Outside in the moonlight, Doyle stopped suddenly on the wooden walkway. Across the road, in front of the grocery store, Satan himself stood. He was looking up at Corey's room, but switched his gaze to Doyle. Red hair, red beard, red plaid jacket. Satan. And his red dog. The Devil Dog. The Hound of Hell. They had been watching Corey's room, not only condoning but encouraging what the football player and Corey had been doing. And now Satan was looking at Doyle, ready to drag him into hell.

"PASTOR!" Doyle screamed loud enough for the whole town to hear him. "PASTOR!"

He ran north on Highway 1 to the dirt road leading down to the homes.

Jessie awoke to a distant cry of "Bastard! Bastard!" It sounded like Doyle. "Oh this god-damn town!" she moaned and turned over. She's leaving tomorrow, not soon enough for her. She'd done her job.

But Jessie, today is Father's Day. And there's one more thing you have to do.

She sat up in bed. What? What? Why won't you tell me?

Peter woke up and looked over at Corey's bed.

"Corey?" he whispered.

"Yeah Pete, that woke you up too?"

"Someone pounding down the stairs, then screaming."

"Just Doyle, having one of his hallucinations. I could hear him sometimes from our home. Dad just tells everyone to ignore him when he gets that way."

"Oh." Peter's mind was made up. He wouldn't spend another night here. He was leaving La Sangre tomorrow, with or without Corey. ("Let's not stop here, Peter," Jay had warned him.) Real or imagined as Jay might be, he should have listened to Jay and kept on driving. He'll leave tomorrow.

But tomorrow—no, today—is Father's Day.

And just what does that mean? Peter wondered, not for the first time that weekend.

"Go back to sleep Pete," Corey said, noticing the protective tone he used. It wasn't lost on Peter either.

"Okay son," Peter said automatically, and wondered why he used that word. Oh stop *thinking* so much Peter, he smiled to himself. Shutup and go back to sleep.

EIGHTEEN

S al stood in the doorway in his boxer shorts. "What do you want Doyle?"

"Pastor..." Doyle faltered. He had never seen the Pastor almost naked before, hadn't known what a solid and compact body he had: short legs with thick calves and massive thighs; no gut at all. Well defined chest, strong arms and shoulders. Just the right amount of black body hair.

Sal wished he had taken the time to put on his robe, but Doyle's screaming for him was worse than it had ever been, and he'd rushed downstairs to the door. But while he was annoyed at Doyle's perusal of his body, he couldn't help but realize that within the past twelve hours, his body had twice been noticed or commented on. He glanced behind him at the stairway; no, three times. "What is it Doyle?"

"Pastor, Satan is loose in La Sangre!"

Sal closed his eyes. He had no one to blame but himself for this kind of talk. Doyle had been getting worse; he noticed it yesterday morning at the gas pumps. Sal had long been using Doyle's weak mind to his own advantage. Was he just now aware of that? "What are you talking about Doyle?"

"Pastor, I saw him. I saw him standing in front of the Grocery Store. He's red. Red hair and beard, red jacket, and even a red dog with him. Red is the devil's color, Pastor, and..."

Doyle stopped, noticing Sal's boxer shorts, white with large red dots on them.

Sal looked down, amused. "Oh these. My wife bought them for me a few years ago. I never wore then until now." Where did this sense of humor come from? Sal wondered; rather, how long has it been gone?

"But worse Pastor, it's that football player."

"What about him?" The ocean air was cold against Sal, and he wanted to end this quickly.

"Pastor, he's..." Doyle stopped.

"Yes?"

Doyle recalled the message he had been given. He'd better stay with the truth, and just recite it word for word. "Pastor, the football player is a homosexual, and he has seduced Corey!"

"Oh for God's sake, Doyle!" It was Doyle's projection, Sal knew it. Sal had enabled that too. He had long seen the irresponsible behavior of the people in La Sangre, but he'd said nothing in order to enable them. Worse, he agreed with their misconceptions to keep them under his control.

"Pastor, it's true. I know."

"What did you see? Don't lie to me Doyle."

"Well...I didn't actually see anything."

"Did you hear anything? In their room?"

Doyle shook his head.

"Then how do you 'know' this?"

"Because God told me, Pastor. And you told me yourself to keep an eye out for Corey."

Sal looked down at the floor. Adultery was the lesser of his sins here in La Sangre. As he and Connie had discussed in the church tonight, they both had a lot of cleaning up to do. He chose his words carefully.

"Doyle, I don't think anything like that happened. Yes, I told you to keep watch over Corey, but he's a smart boy. Naive maybe, and I hold some responsibility for that, but he's old enough to take care of himself."

"But Pastor, God said..."

"Doyle," Sal interrupted, "I've made some very serious mistakes, sins. I was very wrong to tell you to steal Pete's battery out of his truck."

"Pete?"

"The football player. And I was wrong to tell you to lie about no phone calls going out."

And, Sal realized with shame, I was wrong to tell Mary to do the same thing. I've been a liar, and I've told others to lie for me. Lying is one of the worst sins we can commit. It works against the truth. I've got a lot to do.

"But Pastor," Doyle pleaded, "you knew that Satan was coming into La Sangre!"

The Pastor wasn't listening to him, Doyle could see. What's going on? La Sangre is being destroyed by Satan, and the Pastor won't do anything about it!

"I've been very wrong, Doyle, and I have a lot to make up for. I'll talk about it in my sermon tomorrow, if you want to call it a sermon. For now, just go back to bed. I'll talk to Corey tomorrow."

Doyle made an involuntary step backward, his jaw dropping.

"Yes?" Sal asked, anxious to end the conversation. He wondered if the cold he felt was from the salt air or from the magnitude of his sins.

Doyle stared. Satan had gotten into the Pastor too! Satan was indeed in La Sangre, and he went for the obvious target: our Pastor! I have to warn the town.

Yes Doyle. Go warn the town. But don't yell. Be quiet about it.

Doyle couldn't speak. He knew he couldn't talk to or argue with Satan, who was now standing before him. He turned and made himself walk slowly down the steps, away from the Pastor's house.

Sal shut the door. He couldn't go back to sleep. He had a lot of work to do. It may take weeks, months, but he decided to start immediately.

The first light of day woke Corey. He had to go down to the church and ready it for the service. Vacuum, clean the bathrooms. It never took long.

He got up and used the bathroom. He didn't want to shower, at least not until after he cleaned up the church. The noise might wake Pete. Hey, just how much can that guy sleep? But he's been through a lot, I guess he needs his sleep, just like Nurse Walker...Lillian...said.

It was Father's Day, Corey suddenly remembered, and he felt a shot of adrenaline. What's *that* about? True, Father's Day had always been his father's favorite holiday, even more than Christmas and Easter. But this time it was... ominous. Something to be ready for. Prepared.

Finished in the bathroom, Corey quietly went back into the room, dressed noiselessly against Peter's heavy snoring, and quietly went down the stairs.

Doyle also felt a surge of adrenaline during his task as a Christian Paul Revere, going from house to house in La Sangre, banging on the doors. The sun was just coming up, and he knew most everyone would still be asleep, but he also knew they would snap to attention with what he had to tell him.

"Satan has come into La Sangre!" he told Bill and Sadie Parker, who had the house nearest the

Pastor's. "We must all meet at the church to pray for a hedge of protection around this town!"

"I heard you calling for him," Bill Parker said. "Did the Pastor tell you to come see us?"

"No," Doyle said. "Because we have to pray for the Pastor too. He's under attack by Satan."

"Well," Sadie Parker agreed, "he is our Pastor. Satan is always going to be attacking him, more so than the rest of us."

"Yes, but this time it's worse. Hurry. I'll tell the others and see you at the church."

Only Mary, the telephone operator, had any idea of what was going on.

"Doyle," she asked him, in her robe at the front door, "does this have to do with that football player?"

"Yes it does Mary."

"Is he the wolf in sheep's clothing?"

"Yes, but he's only working for the enemy. Satan is here. I saw him, with the football player."

Mary gasped. "I'll wake up Burt."

Sal took a break during his praying and went into the bedroom. Connie was fast asleep. He looked at her tenderly. She was enjoying a good, deep sleep. She deserved it. As much as they'd talked earlier, he hadn't disclosed his adultery, but he knew he would, soon. He'd know the right time to do so. God would see to it, and Sal, at long last, had started listening to Him.

He showered, dressed, and left the house. His first order of business on his long list was to talk to Pete Freeman, of the San Francisco Forty-Niners.

Sal and Corey intercepted each other as they were each crossing the road in front of the gas station.

"Dad, where are you going?"

"I have to talk to Pete. Is he awake?"

Corey shook his ahead. "I just left. I'm going to the church to clean up." Corey looked past his Dad towards the church. "That's funny."

Sal turned and looked. Bill and Sadie Parker were entering the church doors. "What?"

"There's usually one or two people there early, to pray for the service, while I'm cleaning up. But the Parkers never are. They don't show up until the service starts." An idea struck him. "Dad, a few hours ago I heard Doyle pounding down the stairs, screaming for you. Dad, he's crazy."

"I know," Sal sighed, "and I'm partially responsible for that. Doyle needs help, and I'm going to see that he gets it." Sal paused. "And Corey, I want to apologize for the way I behaved yesterday, the things I said. I'm shocked now at how I behaved, taking the Lord's name in vain, calling you what I did. But now I understand it."

"What do you mean?"

"I'll explain later today. I have a lot to tell you. But Corey, I don't think I've been a very good father to you."

Corey stared at him. He hadn't really thought about it one way or the other. It had always been Corey and his mother, and his father was just... just there. And not there. He was wrapped up in the church, in counseling the parishioners, in whatever town business he had to attend to. It had never occurred to Corey that there was something more Sal should have done as a father. Yes, he was shocked at the "goddamn bastard" remark, he'd never heard his father talk that way. But what caused him to do that?

"Dad, I don't..." Corey faltered.

"You don't understand? I know you don't, Corey. And that's my fault too. I love you, and I hope you'll forgive me."

Corey nodded, confused. His father, asking for forgiveness? Who was this man? Is this the first time he saw his father for who he is?

"We'll talk later, okay?" Sal said.

Corey nodded, speechless.

Sal slapped Corey on the left shoulder and walked to the door leading to the stairs of the gas station.

Corey stood in the road. He looked at his left shoulder, still feeling the friendly slap. It was real, it meant something, not like the perfunctory, uncomfortable hugs his father usually gave. And hearing the "I love you?" That had never happened before.

Lillian stared at Doyle in her doorway. "What?"

"Nurse Walker, it's true! Satan is taking over La Sangre!"

Lillian shook her head. *Lord, keep me from slapping this man across the face, but somebody has to.* "What are you talking about Doyle?"

"It's true! You saw it yourself, yesterday, when that football player arrived with Satan! You saw his red truck, red is the devil's color." In confirmation, Doyle was reminded of the Pastor's boxer shorts with the red dots.

And Doyle, what about the shack in McCarthy, Texas, with the red door. You went in that red door and...

Doyle clapped his hands over his ears and screamed "NOOOO!" while Lillian stared at him incredulously. *It's Father's Day,* she suddenly remembered. Either despite or because of Doyle's apparent hallucinations, there was danger today in La Sangre. And she had to get Peter out of here, one way or the other. "I'll be at the church," she told Doyle to get rid of him, and shut the door.

Doyle waited for that voice to stop before removing his hands from his ears. He stood for a moment, and then found the strength to get to the remaining houses.

Peter was half asleep when he heard the quiet rapping on the door.

Who is it? Jay?

The rapping continued.

"Pete? Are you awake?" the voice said.

Where was he? Peter wondered as the dull room materialized and came into focus.

Yes, he was in a room, above the gas station in La Sangre, on the coast. It's Father's Day, and he has to get out. "Yeah, I am now. Who is it?"

The door opened a few inches. "Hi Pete. It's me. Sal Satori."

Corey's father.

"Come on in."

Sal opened the door all the way. "Did I wake you?"

Peter threw the covers back and sat up. "Don't worry about it," he said. The final shroud of sleep disappeared. "I've been sleeping a lot lately."

"I'm Corey's father."

"Yes I know. Pastor Satori."

"Please, call me Sal."

"Sal."

"I'd like to talk to you. No, I *need* to talk to you."

Doyle saved Jessie's house for last, but not just because the Owens' cottage was the furthest south. He relished the idea of knocking on her door. He wanted Jessie to be proud of him, for being the one to recognize Satan, and to bravely gather everyone to pray against the enemy.

Jessie was already dressed when she answered the door.

"Hi Sister Jessie. You're already up!"

She nodded tiredly. "I'm packing. I'm leaving today, remember?"

"Leaving?" Doyle asked, dismayed. She had promised to pray and read the Bible with him. He was certain God had told him that Jessie was to be his wife.

"You knew that Doyle. What do you want?"

"Jessie, Satan is in La Sangre."

Jessie stared at the man. He was pathetic and miserable, but any disparaging remark she may say to him would be way too easy. Still, she couldn't resist.

"I've got news for you Doyle, Satan has long been in La Sangre. The bastard should know."

Doyle faltered. "The Pastor?"

Jessie felt like laughing. "Yes, Doyle."

Doyle responded like he did with the others. He was being wise, he told himself. If the Pastor found out that they all know Satan has him in his taloned grip, it could unleash his fury, the Pastor's and Satan's, since they're now bound together. No, they have to be cautious, as clever as serpents but as gentle as doves.

"Bastard" joke over, Jessie was in her own thoughts. There's still something you have to do, Jessie, that voice told her again. She still didn't know what it was, but maybe Doyle's visit and this "news" might lead to it. "Doyle, how did you find this out, that Satan is here?"

"When that football player arrived yesterday, with Satan."

"I saw the football player, but he was alone," Jessie lied, the same way she had lied to Corey about it. There was no way she was going to admit to anyone about seeing—or thinking she saw—the red-haired stranger seated next to the football player in the Saloon.

Why not Jessie? What are you afraid of?

"No," Doyle said, "I saw Satan with him." He hoped that this revelation would make Jessie see his wonderful gift of discernment. Maybe she'll stay in La Sangre after all, and help him fight the good fight against the evil, by his side, as brother and sister, and as husband and wife. "We're meeting at the church," Doyle said, his excitement rising at what he thought was Jessie's consideration of his vision. "All right?"

"Yes Doyle," Jessie said flatly. She closed the door and stood with her back to it.

Should she go to the church? Or should she just leave? She was almost packed.

"What the *hell* is going on?" she cried out loud.

From outside the cottage the ocean was crashing against the cliff. It seemed to be responding to her question, but she didn't know what it was saying.

Only because you're not listening, Jessie.

Peter sat on the bed, fully awake now, looking at Sal standing in the doorway. The Pastor was a big fan, Corey had told him, not only of the San Francisco Forty-Niners but of Pete Freeman.

"Sure, I'll be happy to talk to you," Peter said politely, in his celebrity sports-figure mode. It wouldn't be the first locker room interview he'd given. "But I need to shit, shave, and shower. Oh, sorry, go to the bathroom."

Sal chuckled. "After what I've done, that's small potatoes."

"Well," Peter got up from the bed, "let me do the first part with the door closed."

"There should be some matches in there."

NINETEEN

After Peter flushed the toilet, lit the match, and washed his hands, he opened the bathroom door to Sal, who was standing outside.

"Well Sal," Peter grabbed his shaving kit, "what can I do for you?"

"I've been wondering about that myself. I guess I just need to talk to a stranger, someone who doesn't know me."

"Yeah, strangers have their uses." Peter covered his face with shaving cream. Just like Jay was a stranger that Peter needed to talk to. He began to shave and waited for Sal to speak.

"Last night I cheated on my wife."

Peter stopped shaving and looked at Sal through the mirror. All right, this wasn't going to be just another locker room interview. "Tell me," he said.

"It was crazy, Pete. It wasn't me. Or maybe it *was* me, and that scares me. I've never done anything like that before. In fact, I didn't even consider it until last September."

"What happened last September?" Peter

kept his voice even and resumed shaving.

"She came into town."

"She?"

"Jessie."

"Jessie?"

"The waitress in the Saloon."

"Oh yeah." Peter had seen how far off she was, how wrong. Interesting that the Pastor hadn't seen it. Shouldn't he be aware of this stuff in his congregation? But if she slept with the Pastor of the town, then something was wrong with her too. It can't be all the Pastor's fault.

While he knew this wasn't going to be another locker room interview, Peter was familiar with the conversation. It was Jeff O'Mahony who had asked Peter to go with him to his first AA meeting, just to hold his hand. Peter was happy to do it, he didn't care who might recognize him there. And if the press got hold of it, Peter knew Jeff was stand-up enough to explain the situation. Even so, Peter had never cared what anyone thought, so he went to two meetings with Jeff, his loyal friend, until Jeff determined he had to man up and stand on his own two feet. ("With God's help," Jeff had told him yesterday, on his three-year anniversary of sobriety.)

"You said," Peter chose his words carefully, "that this was the first time you've done anything like that?"

"Yes."

Peter alternated between watching his shaving and Sal's reflection in the mirror. "All right, so this was the first time. Let me ask you Sal, is it also the last time?"

Sal held Peter's gaze. "Yes. It is."

"Because if you do it again you know it could become a habit."

Sal nodded.

"And a habit," Peter went on, "can become..." He waited.

"An addiction."

Peter nodded at him, his face shaved. "Now, let me shower, and then we'll keep talking." He opened the shower curtain, turned on the faucet, checked the water temperature, dropped his shorts and stepped in.

"All right," Sal said, already feeling lighter.

All the townspeople responded positively to Doyle's alarm. They dressed quickly, woke up their children, bundled up their infants and toddlers and headed for the La Sangre Christian Church. Inside, they whispered quietly and reverently, waiting for the Pastor. All they knew, they told each other, was that Satan was loose in the town, and they must band together and pray. Some of them wondered if it had anything to do with that football player who had come into town. They knew he couldn't be a Christian, not playing football with all the attendant parties and drink and drugs and sex.

Yes, maybe the football player was a wolf in sheep's clothing, because the Pastor had told the few who had cars not to give him a ride out of town. And Mary the Operator confided in them that the Pastor had ordered her not to let the football player make any outbound calls. Oh no, she reminded one of them, the football player can't get access to the switchboard. He wouldn't even know how to work it.

So, the football player is Satan in the flesh, is he? one woman asked her friend.

I don't know, her friend answered, but the Pastor will explain.

But where *is* the Pastor? the first one asked. He has to be here to lead us in prayer. He's our leader, our shepherd.

Don't worry, the other woman said. He'll be here, and he'll make everything all right again.

Doyle had been standing at the door, greeting everyone, imbued with an authority and confidence he hadn't thought possible. Thank you Lord, he said to himself, for leading me correctly.

Finally everyone was there, except for Nurse Walker...and Jessie! Where was Jessie? Doyle wondered. He wanted her to see him, the real Doyle, doing the Lord's work. But the anxious whispers were getting louder, telling him he had no choice but to proceed. He walked up the aisle and stood behind the pulpit.

The whispers increased in volume at seeing Doyle at the venerable place used only by the Pastor. They had indeed noticed and even remarked to each other about Doyle's stalwart presence at the door. That was strange, but stranger yet, what is Doyle doing up there? He's a faithful servant, yes, but he's kind of dumb, God bless him.

The whispers ceased abruptly when Doyle opened his mouth to speak.

"Thank you, brothers and sisters, for responding to the call so faithfully." Doyle felt a new confidence in his voice, a new authority. Oh where was Jessie, so she could see this? "I have called you all here because of an attack upon La Sangre by the enemy," he paused for emphasis, "Satan!"

A few cries rose from the congregation. Women held their lap children tightly to their bosoms, the men looked at each other in stern anticipation of battle.

"At this very moment, our very own Pastor is battling with the enemy, struggling to defeat Satan," Doyle continued, his adrenaline surging at the response. This could be just the beginning. Should Satan deliver the final blow to the Pastor, why Doyle himself might even become...

"The Pastor!" one of the men interrupted Doyle. "Where is the Pastor? Doesn't he need us to join him in the battle?"

Think Doyle. Keep your head. It's too soon to announce that the Pastor has indeed fallen prey to the devil. "It is not for us to know or understand the details of the battle between the Pastor and Satan," Doyle rallied, "it is only for us to band together as Christian soldiers, armed for battle, to pray for the Pastor and to pray for La Sangre, to bring Satan to his knees in the agony of defeat!"

The congregation responded with shouts of Amens and hallelujahs.

"Let us pray," Doyle bowed his head.

Shortly after Doyle had left her house, Lillian went to the Satori house, where she found Corey and Connie on the deck.

"*What* is going on?" she asked them as she came up the stairs.

Connie shook her head, arms folded, watching the ocean.

"Oh, Doyle's going crazy," Corey answered. "He's been running around like a madman, warning everyone that Satan is loose in La Sangre, and to meet at the church for prayer."

Lillian didn't mention Doyle's bizarre hands-over-his-ears behavior. It wasn't necessary. "Yes," she said. "That's what he told me."

"He was here," Connie said, "just before dawn. I overheard him telling Sal that Satan was in town."

It was all coming together somehow, Lillian thought. Peter Freeman comes into town and suddenly Doyle, pathetic Doyle, has everyone pumped up about Satan. But wait, Peter hadn't been alone. Peter had told her that a man named Jay Carpenter was with him, a man that apparently nobody else had seen. Corey and Connie hadn't seen this mysterious figure. Had Sal?

"Did Doyle say he actually saw Satan?" Lillian asked.

"That's what he told Sal," Connie said, wanting this day, this weekend, to be over.

"Did Doyle say what he looked like?" Lillian asked.

"Something about him being all red," Connie said, "with red hair, red beard, and a red flannel jacket. Oh, and a red dog."

Lillian looked at Corey. "That's just how Peter described Jay Carpenter." It was coming together, but not yet solid. "Where is Sal now?"

"I just saw him," Corey said, "in town. He said he was going to talk to Pete about something."

"Something's coming together, I just don't know what it is yet," Lillian said. "Let's go to the church, see what Doyle's talking about."

"I did everything I was told to do," Sal said while Peter toweled himself dry. "I was a good kid, obeyed all the rules. I didn't even jay-walk.

No trouble at all, an easy kid to raise. Even my Dad had to admit that."

Peter stopped drying off and looked at Sal. He too, had been a good kid, he realized for the very first time. He'd never been told that, at least not by his father. He proceeded to scrub his hair dry as Sal went on.

"But that meant I couldn't make friends with the other boys, at least not in school, and there was no one my age in our church."

"Catholic?"

"No. Both my parents are Italian, but for some reason they left the Catholic Church and went Protestant, a small, conservative church. And like I say, no one my age to make friends with."

"Like Corey has it now," Peter commented.

"Yeah, like Corey has it now," Sal nodded. "But at least Corey, being alone here, doesn't have to do what I did: walk away when the other boys started telling dirty jokes or getting into mischief, the things kids do. I tried to make friends, but when I'd walk up to them, they'd shutup, and disperse. So I cut myself off from them, the neighborhood kids, the school kids, even though I didn't want to. It's part of playing by the rules, you can't listen to that stuff or join in. But it hurt because...I wanted the boys, my age, to like me. But they didn't."

"Did you play any sports?"

"Yeah, but I was mediocre at best. If not the last chosen, close to it. All I was really good at was boxing."

Peter sized him up. "Yeah, you're built like it."

"I was comfortable in the ring, at the Boys Club. When the gloves were put on me, and I got into that ring, I felt at home. We just did three one-minute rounds, but with those gloves on, I could take my swings and know I couldn't really hurt them. I beat everyone. Their swings were predictable. I'd just block them and wait for my opening, and then go in." He looked at Peter. "Like you did on the football field. You always found your opening."

Peter nodded. He hung the towel over the curtain rod and put on a fresh pair of shorts.

"Pete?"

"Yeah?"

"I just realized that I played by the rules—in everything, even in boxing—so that God would like me! That's why I went into the ministry. So *God* would like me! But...but I don't think He ever did! *Like* me!"

("Yeah, welcome to the 'You'll-Never-Be-Good-Enough' club.") That's what Jay had told Peter, and Peter knew that what Sal was saying applied to both of them. Different in some ways, yet basically the same. "I'll get dressed," was all Peter could respond. Sal followed him back into Corey's room.

"Heavenly Father," Doyle's voice rang through the church, but then stopped as Lillian, Connie, and Corey came in and sat in the back pew. The Pastor's wife is here (but still no Jessie). He'd better be careful about what he said, how he prayed. Doyle resumed his prayer. "We pray for a hedge of protection from Satan around La Sangre, around all of us gathered here, around our Pastor. Protect him Lord. Protect us, our town, and our Pastor, from Satan!"

Sal sat on Corey's bed while Peter dressed. "I never drank. I wouldn't know pot if I saw it, or smelled it. I liked some popular music but never bought the records. I didn't go to R-Rated movies. I'd still like to see 'The Godfather.' People used to call me that, you know, because of my Italian heritage." He paused and smiled. "They weren't wrong, especially given the way I've behaved around here."

"Your parents were against all that stuff?"

"No, that's what's strange. None of this was foisted on me. They listened to their music, the big band stuff, Sinatra, Tony Bennett, all of that. They'd dance in the living room, dance at weddings. They weren't as conservative as most of the people in our church. Both being Italian, they drank wine, but I didn't touch it. It was my own rules I was setting for myself."

"Pretty tight rules." Peter put on his shirt.

"What about girls?"

"I dated once or twice, if you want to call it dating. Usually it meant escorting a girl to a Bible study. I was a virgin on my wedding night. Always playing by the rules. Always. When I met Connie she told me, right up front, that she was already pregnant, from some guy she knew in high school. She said it was a one-time thing, he was the only one. She hadn't expected it to happen."

Peter froze as he was tucking in his shirt. He stared at Sal. It was true. He knew it. He probably knew it yesterday. ("Go back to sleep Pete," Corey had said. "Okay son.")

Sal could have read the expression on Peter's face, but he was looking down at the floor. "It didn't matter to me that she was pregnant," he was saying, "and I told Connie so at the time; at least I *thought* it didn't matter. But when Corey was born, I knew that it did matter. I...I couldn't be a real father to him."

Dumbfounded, Peter managed to finish tucking in his shirt. "Did your wife tell you...who Corey's father is?"

"No, and I didn't ask her"

Peter slowly grabbed his shoes and socks and sat down on the bed. Sal was still looking at the floor. "Sal, did Connie tell you about me, in high school?"

"Yes, and I guess that's what led me to be a

fan. There was a connection. But then it's like I became, well, fixated on you, not like just a fan but a fanatic. Pete, you were like the guys I grew up with, that I wanted to *like* me. I'd watch the great Pete Freeman run down the field, scoring a touchdown, and I just thought you were the greatest running back in NFL history. And I wanted you to *like* me."

"Well Sal, that's what fans are like," Peter said. "They think we're, I don't know, some kind of gods out there on the field. You know that Patton and Cooper got more yardage than I did, but they're not gods either."

Sal finally looked up at Peter. "But they ran close to the ground, not like you ran."

"What does that mean?"

"When you'd run down the field, Pete, carrying that ball, I thought that with every step you'd sprout wings, and fly right over that goal post. The ultimate touchdown. It's what I wanted to do for myself, through you. I wanted to score the ultimate touchdown. Instead, I feel like I've failed at everything I've done, or tried to do. I've failed my wife, my son, my congregation. How can I continue with that?"

"Lord, give us the strength," Doyle continued to pray. "Let us not be afraid, knowing You can cast off all demons, all the evil that this world has to offer. Let us march forward bravely, afraid of nothing, knowing that You are our Protector."

"This is the hard part," Sal told Peter, who was dressed and now knew he was Corey's father. It was true. A simple, plain, fact of his life. "When you walked into the Saloon yesterday, I wanted to," Sal took a deep breath, "I wanted to walk up to you and introduce myself and invite you to stay the weekend, at my home. Come to church if you wanted, come to the picnic afterward."

"Why didn't you?" Peter inquired. He received a lot of invitations like that from people he didn't know. Some he accepted, most he turned down. But he admitted to himself that he didn't know if he would have accepted Sal's invitation or not. Oh yes he would have, for the kid. For his son.

"That would have been fine, Sal," Peter said after a moment, still shallow-breathed, "to ask me, I mean."

"But I couldn't!" Sal's voice rose.

"Why not?"

"Because I was afraid of being rejected! And worse, I wouldn't have known how to ask you. Pete, I don't know how to talk to people, just *preach* to them!"

Lillian started. She knew God speaking to her. No mistake. "I'm going up to the General

Store," she whispered to Connie and Corey.

"I'll go with you," Corey said. He sensed the urgency in her voice.

"I'm going to stay here for a while," Connie told them, "to keep praying." All through Doyle's long, passionate, and yes, well-intentioned and guided prayer, Connie understood that it's not about the vessel. That vessel could be as clean or dirty or smart or dumb as you please; after all, God had chosen to use an ass to speak to Balaam, hadn't He? Was Doyle—or am I—any different? It's about the intent, about the heart, and whatever was going on in La Sangre, God was hearing Doyle's, our, prayers.

Sal was changing, Connie was changing, and now she needed to pray for Peter, and for their son, Corey. "I have to stay here," she told Lillian and Corey. She couldn't walk out now. She was, after all, the Pastor's wife, and she had a duty to stay there.

Lillian and Corey both nodded—Lillian thoroughly understanding—and they left.

"So what I did," Sal said to Peter, "oh God, I'm ashamed to admit this to you Pete." His head was down to his chest.

"Go on Sal."

"I told..." Sal took a deep breath. "I told Doyle to steal your battery, so you'd have to stay here for a while, so maybe I could work up the nerve to talk to you. I also told Mary, the operator, to lie to you that no calls can go out." Sal paused, he couldn't look at Pete Freeman of the San Francisco Forty-Niners any more; he continued to look at the floor. "What amazes me, no, what scares me, is how I got these people, my own congregation, to lie and steal at my bidding. They didn't even question it! That's how far under my control I have...had them." He finally looked up at Peter...interestingly, he now saw a man sitting there, not the Running Back for the Forty-Niners. "I've got a lot to answer for Pete, and lying and stealing from you is just a part of it. I have to answer to God, and to the law. So what I want you to do is call the Sheriff. I know God will forgive me, I pray you will, but now I have to accept legal responsibility for what I did. I *want* to."

The theft of his truck battery was totally irrelevant, Peter thought. Or maybe totally relevant. It had allowed me to meet Corey. To meet my son.

"Pete, did you hear me? We're going to call the Sheriff. I have a private line at my house, no one knows that."

Corey was all Peter could think about. "Hey man," he reached out and squeezed Sal's knee, "it had to happen that way. I'm glad it happened that way."

"What? Why?"

"Sal...you have to know this, and I just realized it myself. I knew Connie, your wife, in high school. But there's more to it than what she told you."

Pastor Salvatore Satori and San Francisco 49er Pete Freeman looked at each other. It was trust and warmth, brother to brother. Nothing had to be said. When words fail, the eyes can speak, and for Peter Freeman and Sal Satori, stripped of their titles and positions, their blue and dark brown eyes spoke volumes.

By now sunlight was flooding into the dingy room above the La Sangre Last Chance Gas Station and Garage.

"You know," Sal finally broke the silence. "I *knew* that, that you were Corey's father. I think I knew that just by watching you play football, and watching Corey grow. I mean I *knew* it but yet I *didn't*. I guess that's why I reacted the way I did when you walked into the Saloon, snapping at Corey and calling him what I did. I had to have known. And maybe Corey knows too, I don't know."

"I don't think he does, yet. But you and I will tell him, together, all right?"

Sal nodded. "And with Connie present. She's his Mom."

"Of course. Let's find them and do this."

"But Pete, you're going to call the Sheriff. I want you to."

"No," Peter said.

"Why not?" Sal asked.

"Stealing someone's battery?" Peter smiled. "Small potatoes."

Sal held his gaze on Peter. "God brought you here, didn't he?"

Peter nodded. "It sure seems like it." But why was Jay determined that Peter leave, not to stop in La Sangre? It made no sense; it was a missing piece that would complete the picture.

Sal shook his head, amazed. "Pete, we're so *dumb*, aren't we? Men, I mean."

"Yeah Sal. That's how we can play football."

"And box," Sal chuckled. "Come on, let's go get your battery."

Lillian and Corey left the church and headed towards town. The prayer time in the church had revitalized Lillian. Funny, she'd expected to have a good laugh at Doyle, but found herself in one of the best communications with God she'd had in months, maybe years. Like Connie, she realized the instrument of prayer is unimportant. She'd put too much emphasis on people, and had ignored God, mistrusting Him as yet another man who would only desert her, discoloring God with her own fears and prejudices. Maybe Doyle—for all his hangups—maybe he at least chose to see God as real and sovereign and uncomplicated. Neurotic and unhappy and misguided as Doyle may be, at least he prayed, at least he trusted, at least he believed that God would be faithful, right to the end. That was something Lillian had stopped believing long ago.

All Jessie knew, all she had left to hold onto, was that she had to get out of La Sangre, quickly, unfinished business or not. The car was packed, the canvas roof was down. She wanted to drive south on Highway 1, top down, and even without a seat belt, simulating free flight along the Pacific Ocean as best as she could. Yes, she wanted to fly. She had always wanted to fly, needed to fly. Since she was a child. Fly away from her father's house. Like the song, and yes, that was one good thing about church, she discovered her favorite song was "I'll Fly Away." She got in the car and started the engine. Yes, she'll fly away, out of La Sangre forever.

But where to after this Jessie? Where are you going? Aren't you tired yet?

"And now brothers and sisters," Doyle said to the congregation, "let us all recite the prayer that our Lord taught us. 'Our Father, who art in heaven, hallowed be thy name.'"

Lillian and Corey approached town just as Sal and Peter came out of the gas station. Sal was carrying a car battery.

"Dad?" Corey called.

Sal and Peter responded in unison to the call. Lillian stopped in her tracks. They know; yes, they both know. She watched while Corey crossed the road to them. Which one would he go to?

The congregation had joined Doyle in the prayer. "Thy Kingdom come, Thy will be done..."

Jessie made the right turn from the dirt road onto Highway 1, going as fast as she could without losing the turn. As soon as all four tires were on asphalt, she hit the gas.

"...on Earth as it is in Heaven."

When Jessie saw Corey crossing the road, she had her very last moment of sanity, of clarity. She saw Corey. The beauty and the innocence. The trust and love. She hated it, she hated all of it, the beauty in particular, and she needed to destroy it. Beauty was enigmatic, it could and would leave you in a moment. Or it could be robbed from you, as her beauty, and her innocence and trust, had been robbed from her. So she'd spent her life in retaliation, in her quest to destroy beauty whenever and wherever she could. She knew how to do it, and that was all she had. It was all she ever had. All she'd been left with. All she was good at. The need, the drive, to destroy beauty.

"'Give us this day our daily bread....'"

"Corey!" Peter screamed, seeing Jessie's car bearing down on him.

Corey stopped in the middle of the road. If I hadn't screamed, Peter realized, too late, Corey might have kept walking and the black sports car would have missed him. But no, even then, the way the sports car was purposefully bearing down on him, it would have followed Corey as its target.

"..and forgive us our trespasses..."

At the final second, Jessie would have sworn that it was her right foot, on its own, that had shoved the accelerator to the floor. She hadn't willed her foot to do that, she was sure of that; it had operated of its own accord. It wasn't her.

It wasn't *her*!

"...as we forgive those who trespass against us."

Pete Freeman wasn't the greatest tackler in the NFL, but playing for the offense, he didn't have to be. It was just for interceptions anyway, and Quarterback Joe Montana had among the lowest interception rates in NFL history. So Peter would tackle when he had to, and he never incurred a penalty.

This time though, Pete Freeman would have been penalized. He burst with energy and took five long strides, then catapulted his body, twisted it horizontally, and slammed Corey below the buttocks, sending Corey into one of the posts of the Grocery Store.

Then the black sports car was upon Peter.

"And lead us not into temptation..."

As Jessie's car continued to the sharp left turn just past the General Store, she cried out "GOD, WHY DID YOU LET ME DO THAT? WHY DIDN'T YOU STOP ME?" The car hit the steel guard rail, collapsing and catapulting Jessie out of her seat, over what was left of the front end, over the guard rail, and down to the rocks and salt water. The car horn spread an interminable high-pitched scream throughout La Sangre.

"...but deliver us from evil."

Corey landed just a few feet from where Lillian was standing. She began to crouch to him but was stopped by a tall man, a big man, with red hair and a red beard, wearing a red plaid jacket.

"His left femur is snapped," the man told her. "I'll handle it."

"Do you know how to set a broken bone?" Lillian asked him, knowing immediately that he did.

"Yes. Go see to Peter."

"What about the girl?"

"She's dead. Go see to Peter."

Lillian ran over to Peter as the man knelt by Corey's feet. "Okay Corey," he instructed, "I want you to put your head back, and look up at the sky, and when I say scream, I want you to scream as loud as you can, all right?"

In impossible pain, Corey nodded.

The man grabbed Corey's left knee. "Okay Corey, NOW, SCREAM!"

"AAAAGGHH!" Corey screamed as the man made a strong, steady pull.

"Okay Corey," he grabbed Corey's left ankle, "one more time. SCREAM!"

"DA-DEEEEEEEEEEE!"

"'For Thine is the Kingdom, and the Power, and the Glory....'"

Lillian stood over Sal, who was sitting in the middle of the road, holding Peter in his arms.

Peter's mid-section was crushed. The internal bleeding would be profuse. Lillian knew he'd be dead before she could reach the phone.

"Sal?" Peter looked up at him, fear and loneliness in his eyes.

"I've got you Pete," Sal told him. "Stay with me."

"Corey?"

"He's all right. Some guy is with him. He looks like a doctor."

Both of Peter's lungs were punctured, blood quickly filling them. He managed to say "...big guy...red beard..."

"Yeah," Sal said. "That's him."

"Sal...did you...see me?"

"I saw you Pete, and you were great. Thank you. I love you."

Peter managed a nod and tried for one last word, but instead his final exhale sent the blood in his lungs exploding from his mouth, covering Sal's chest. Sal kept holding him. It was over.

...forever. Amen."

The pain was gone, the screaming car horn had stopped.

All Peter could hear was the sound of the ocean. No seagulls. Peaceful. The ocean was his, at last. He opened his eyes and saw Jay standing over him.

"Jay?"

"Come on Peter," he nodded. "Let's go North."

Peter gratefully held up his right hand. Jay reached down with a strong right arm and pulled him up.

TWENTY

A hero's funeral was planned for Peter Freeman at his home town of Bakersfield. Two days before the funeral, Sal, Connie, and Corey Satori drove down to Bakersfield to meet Mrs. Grace Freeman. During the drive to Bakersfield the Satoris talked, and prayed, about how they would handle the situation. This was a woman who within ten days had lost the two men in her life, her husband and her only son. And losing a child, Lillian had advised the Satoris, on both her nurse's and personal experience, was the worst thing in life that could happen to a woman, to anyone.

When the Satoris arrived at the Freeman home and introduced themselves, Mrs. Freeman remembered their phone call and welcomed them into her home. Sal and Connie sat on the long couch in the living room, Mrs. Freeman faced them in a large wing chair, and Corey sat between them in his wheelchair.

Connie carefully told Mrs. Freeman about her wonderful history with Peter, her trials as a child and Peter always being nice to her, even asking her to dance. During the part where Peter had defended Connie on the school bus, Mrs. Freeman teared up and said, "Yes, that was like Peter to do that. He was always that way. Remember, he had four little sisters to protect."

Then, slowly and quietly, Connie told Mrs. Freeman of her one date with Peter and what had happened.

There was silence, Mrs. Freeman digesting the information. After a minute, Sal got up and walked to Corey, putting his hand on Corey's shoulder. "Mrs. Freeman, I'd like you to meet Pete's son, your grandson, Corey Peter Satori."

There was more silence while everything was taken in by Mrs. Freeman, and then tears flowed, followed by hugs and recognition. "I had a flash of Peter when I first saw Corey," she cried, "even in the wheelchair. I must have known, somehow."

Mrs. Freeman wasn't shocked, Connie noticed gratefully; she welcomed this unexpected news as a joyous gift to a grieving woman.

"You've given me so much!" Mrs. Freeman cried as she hugged Connie.

"Like Peter gave to me," Connie told her tearfully. "To all of us."

The funeral was well attended by Peter's former teammates, as well as by a few of their Rivals-Across-The-Bay, the Oakland Raiders. Per Mrs. Freeman's request, Corey parked his wheelchair next to her in the front pew.

On the drive back from Bakersfield, the Satoris stopped at Santa Cruz to look at Bethany Bible College, which Corey had decided to attend in the fall; in fact, he was enthusiastic about it, to Sal and Connie's relief. Sal had been concerned that Corey would feel obligated due to the scholarship, but Corey convinced him it was what he wanted. Corey explained "Dad, it's what I want. Plus I'm doing it for you and my other Dad, Pete Freeman." Sal, Connie and Corey knew that Corey's getting the scholarship offer on Father's Day weekend was not seren-dipitous. And now Peter was Dad, Sal was still Dad, and the Satori family was reborn.

The forgiveness of Sal's adultery came easier than either Sal or Connie would have thought possible, mainly because Connie told Sal that she was, in her way, committing adultery during their marriage: being in love with—or *thinking* she was in love with—someone else, and not even making an attempt to get to know Sal, her husband. Moreover, both Sal and Connie had to deal with something even worse: their guilt. Sal

felt responsible for Peter's death; if only he had
let Peter leave La Sangre, he'd be alive. Connie
was certain she should have told Peter, and Sal,
about Corey's birthright years ago. Forgiving
themselves of their perceived responsibilities in
the tragedy put the adultery into perspective. It
would all take time.

The day after they returned to La Sangre,
Sal was sitting alone on the bench outside the
Grocery Store, looking at the red stain in the
middle of Highway 1. Already it was being
worn away by the traffic, and Sal hoped that
some remnant of it would always be there,
at least until the road had to be repaved. He
was thinking of a scene with Doyle on Father's
Day afternoon. After the State Police had in-
terviewed the witnesses and written their report, and the ambulances had left with the two
bodies, Doyle had gone out into the middle of
the road with a bucket of soap and water and
a wire brush to clean up the blood. Sal ran out
to stop him.

"What are you doing Doyle?" Sal had fairly
screamed at him.

"Pastor, we have to clean up this mess!"
Doyle replied, surprised.

"It's *my* mess Doyle. I'm responsible for it."

"Okay Pastor, if you say so," and he handed
the bucket and brush to Sal.

"No, I mean I'm responsible for all this happening!"

"Pastor, how are you..."

"Doyle, I'll be discussing that in church, in our Bible studies, in our prayer time. And you and I will talk alone about some things. But not right now, all right?"

Doyle at first thought that maybe the Pastor's wish for a private conference was to offer him an Associate Pastorship. But no, not the way the Pastor was looking at him, and he suddenly became afraid.

"Doyle, we have to grow as Christians, we have to face our pasts, our fears, our insecurities. It's scary, I know, but it's scriptural. We can't live in..." Sal swept his arm around La Sangre, "...in a fog. We have to wake up, and grow up."

Dejected, Doyle walked back to the La Sangre Garage, hoping that the familiarity of his routine, the gas station, his room above it, would comfort him. He threw out the soapy water, rinsed the bucket and attended to his chores. All his life he'd moved westward, escaping McCarthy, Texas. But now he was at the Pacific Ocean, and he could go no further.

As Sal sat on the bench, remembering that scene with Doyle, he also wondered how cooperative Doyle would be seeing a psychiatrist. Sal wasn't trained to deal with whatever trauma Doyle must have experienced as a child. He had tried to explain to Doyle that counseling was scriptural, and that he would be there to hold Doyle's hand throughout it. They'd talk about the recurring nightmares that Doyle was having, and he may discover it is a path to his healing.

Through this, and with his interactions with the other townspeople, Sal was beginning to understand that it was his job as a Pastor not to *drive* his flock, but to lead them.

Inside the General Store, Lillian busied herself. Her missing Peter would come unexpectedly in a huge wave, and then subside for a while. Right now she felt one of those waves swelling over her head as she was sweeping the floor. The wave subsided when she thought of the paramedic from Santa Rosa who had asked her if she was the one who had set Corey's left femur so neatly. Lillian told him no, but sometimes bones automatically re-set themselves, don't they? It sounded dumb, she knew, especially for a nurse, but the paramedic just said he'd report that to the attending doctor. Corey was in too much pain to answer the paramedic's questions, then he was sedated, and later, he couldn't remember anything, other than the fact that his father, Pete Freeman, as Sal and Connie had told him, had given his life for him.

Still sitting on the bench, staring at the blood stain in the road, Sal said to himself "We could have been great friends, Pete."

"You *are* great friends," said a voice next to him.

Sal turned to his right and wasn't surprised to see the hitchhiker, cop, doctor, whatever he was, seated next to him.

"Thank you for setting Corey's bone," Sal said.

"Lillian could have done it. There was just so much going on I thought I'd help out."

Sal looked back at the blood stain. "I don't know if I can do this. Connie has forgiven me, the town seems to have forgiven me, God has forgiven me. But..."

"Yes?"

"But I can't forgive myself."

"You know Sal, sometimes I just want to slap you. Like Brando slapped that singer in 'The Godfather.'"

"I've really got to see that movie," Sal muttered.

"The point is, will you just shutup and let me do my job?"

"All right," Sal turned to him. "But I'll take responsibility for my behavior, and I won't use you as an excuse."

"And I won't let you."

Oh, she'll clean the store later, Lillian decided. She set the broom down and walked outside for some fresh air, and saw Sal sitting by himself on the bench in front of the Grocery Store, looking at the blood stain in the road. She walked over to him.

"Hi Lillian," Sal said as she approached.

"Hi Sal." Lillian sat down on the bench.

"Lillian, are you going anywhere?" he asked her.

"I was just going to walk down to the ocean. I'll get someone to watch the store for me."

"Never mind, I'll keep an eye on it. But I meant, are you going to leave? Leave La Sangre?"

Lillian looked at him. "I was thinking about it. But no, I'm not."

"I'm glad. I need you here."

"I belong here Sal. This is my home. It's finally become my home. Funny, the lessons we hear as kids but don't really understand. Do you remember 'The Wizard Of Oz?'"

"Yeah, I allowed myself to watch it. It wasn't rated 'R.'"

Lillian smiled at Sal's newfound sense of humor. "At the end of the movie, the Scarecrow asks Dorothy, 'What have you learned?' And Dorothy says 'If I ever go looking for my heart's desire, I won't look any further than my own back yard.' I really didn't have to leave La Sangre to learn what I did."

Sal looked at her. "Are you sure? I've been wondering about that myself. I don't know if I would have learned what I did if I hadn't behaved so badly. It's like the Prodigal Son; did he *have* to leave home to learn what he did? Would he have learned it if he'd just stayed home?"

"Well, we have to leave home some time."

"Our physical home maybe, but not our heart." The chorus to "Tin Man," a song by America that Sal had long forgotten, came to him like joyful confirmation, as if straight from the Bible itself.

Sal chuckled. "Lillian, you may have just written my next sermon."

Lillian smiled and patted his knee, then got up and walked north to the road leading down to the bluff. She needed to look at the ocean so she could relive and cherish the brief time she'd spent with Peter, and the magic he had brought to La Sangre.

At the junction of the highway and the dirt road stood the six-foot-five, red-haired, red-bearded man with the red plaid jacket. The Irish Setter sat next to him, looking up at the man, and then at Lillian.

Lillian didn't hesitate, she walked right up to him. She had hoped she would see him again, at least once.

"Hi Lillian," he extended his hand. "Are you doing okay?"

"Just." What big hands he has, she noticed, and surprisingly soft. "I needed a break. I'm going to walk down to the cliff."

"May I join you?"

"Please."

As they walked down the dirt road, Barney saw the seagulls flying over the ocean and ran down to them, barking.

"Watch that cliff Barney!" he warned. He and Lillian didn't speak until they reached the cliff.

"There are a million things I'd like to ask you," Lillian said.

"Go ahead."

"I don't understand what you told Peter about being a Los Angeles policeman, having a nervous breakdown, all of that."

"I had to relate to Peter at a place where he was at. Things always came rather easily for him, he never had to make any major decisions. But his great sensitivity was a sharp contrast to his athletic prowess and powerful body. After football, he was trying to figure out what he was going to do, and then his father's early death coercing him into taking over the company..." He shook his head. "Lawrence Freeman Produce would have killed Peter."

"Like it did his father?"

"Well, at least his father loved what he was doing. But Peter wasn't built for it, and just thinking about it was taking him towards a breakdown. Like that undercover cop whose in-basket was overflowing, Peter was feeling buried and helpless."

"And then you found him, at the Golden Gate Bridge."

"Or he found me. But as far as telling him I was a cop, I actually have been that cop." He paused for a moment, looking out at the ocean. "I've been a lot of things."

Lillian considered everything he said. It made sense, except... "Peter said you warned him to leave La Sangre when you first arrived. Was he wrong not to leave?"

He turned back to her. "It's true I advised him to leave, but it was his choice to stay. I respect that."

"But he'd still be alive today, if he had left."

He shrugged. "For a while."

Lillian smiled. "The way you say 'for a while,' it doesn't sound like very long."

"It isn't, really."

This was incredible, Lillian thought. All these answers. I could ask anything. "But if Peter had left town he wouldn't have met Corey, his son. No wait, Connie told me that she was planning on telling Sal and Corey who his father was, as soon as Corey was 18. They would have met after that."

He nodded.

"And what about Jessie?' Lillian asked. "Was

she...saved?"

"That's between me and her."

"Oh of course," Lillian sighed, feeling dumb. "It's really none of my business."

"There's just so much of that, Lillian, a whole history of it." He glanced behind him at the town. "People running around, worrying and wondering, 'Is he saved, is she saved? He or she can't be a Christian if he or she does this or that.' But it's not what you do, it's who you are. And 'whose' you are."

"I'm yours," Lillian said softly, and he nodded and smiled in acceptance. "By the way, thank you for protecting me through Seattle. You must have been speaking to me, but I didn't listen."

"You were young and silly, Lillian."

"Young and dumb you mean."

"Young and *silly*. Do you remember what you did when you got to the fairgrounds and saw that Matthew had left you?"

Lillian flashed back to standing at the fairgrounds, lost and empty. "Yes, I do remember what I did. I prayed. I also remember thinking that it had been a long time since I'd done so."

He smiled at her. "Lillian, prayer is so powerful, it makes all things possible, including, and especially, love. And love, that's the most important thing of all."

"I still don't know what love is," Lillian said,

thinking of her conversation with Connie.

"Yes you do. Do you remember what I said once: 'Greater love has no one than this: than...' Than to *what* Lillian?"

"'Than to lay down one's life for his friends.' Like Peter did for Corey?"

"Well that was rather exceptional, and those opportunities don't often come along. No, 'laying down your life' is more commonly like how Connie laid down her life to you, in her kitchen, how you laid down your life to Peter and Corey over dinner, how Sal laid down his life to Peter, how Connie laid down her life to Peter's mother."

He looked out to where the ocean ended at the sky, remembering something that had happened to him two thousand years ago, on the other side of the world. "It was so simple," he said. "I wanted them to see just how simple it could be, how easy." He again glanced back at La Sangre. "I never wanted it to become like this."

"Maybe now that you're here," Lillian said, "finally here, it doesn't have to be that way anymore."

"I hope so. That's up to everyone here."

"But what about Satan? I mean, he *is* real, isn't he?"

He nodded soberly. "Yes, but don't overdo it. Certainly be advised and be careful, pray and stay guided, use discernment. But ultimately I can handle him."

"Some people here thought that you were Satan."

He chuckled. "It's not an uncommon mistake. I'm used to it. And yes, the truth can be frightening and confusing. But it sets you free."

Lillian followed his gaze out to the ocean, the horizon. It was so big, so infinite, and even frightening in a way. And yet it was so simple. How could people—how could she—have made it so impossible? She turned back to him.

"What about me? What's going to happen?"

"What do *you* want, Lillian?"

"I guess...I guess I just don't want to be alone anymore. I want to find someone. Maybe even get married."

"That's up to you."

"It *is* possible then! That's what I needed to hear. I'd given up on it."

He looked into Lillian's eyes, knowing her, loving her. "Don't give up, Lillian. With God all things are possible."

Lillian smiled up at him. This was happiness. Pure, total, real happiness. All the time, every day, no matter what happens. Happiness. "Will you...do me a favor?"

"Name it."

"Please hold me."

"Of course," he smiled. He put his arms around her and she rested her head against his chest.

"God, you *are* real," she whispered.

He held her for as long as she wanted. When she pulled back he kept his arm around her shoulders as they watched the ocean together, while Barney barked at seagulls along the cliff.

CPSIA information can be obtained
at www.ICGtesting.com
Printed in the USA
BVOW06*1849240417
481051BV00018B/191/P